Creative Dramatics for Children

A Practical Manual
for Teachers and Leaders

NEW EDITION

FRANCES CALDWELL DURLAND

THE KENT STATE UNIVERSITY PRESS

Copyright © 1952, 1975 by The Kent State University Press

Library of Congress Cataloging in Publication Data
Durland, Frances Caldwell.
    Creative dramatics for children.
    Bibliography: p.
    1. Drama in education.   2.   Improvisation (Acting)
3.   Children's plays—Presentation, etc.   I.   Title.
[PN3171.D8   1975]   792'.07'1   75-1493
ISBN 0-87338-175-0 pbk.

Library of Congress Catalog Card Number 75-1493
ISBN 0-87338-175-0
Manufactured in the United States of America

Table of Contents

Introduction to the New Edition 1

Foreword 7

1 Creative Dramatics 10

2 Source Material for Creative Dramatics . . . 19

3 Technique of the Story Drama 24

4 Psychological and Behavior Patterns 55

5 Specific Rehearsal Problems 68

6 Creative Directing 82

7 Suitable Dramatic Material 98

8 Analysis of Stories 108

9 Research in Creative Dramatics 126

10 Creative Teaching 135

Appendix—Group A 145

Appendix—Group B 166

Bibliography 180

Introduction to the New Edition

A number of years ago, in a college workshop class in play direction, I urged my students to experiment with various directing techniques. One day a student who was directing a scene from a fast-moving farce brought a small bean bag to his rehearsal. I was curious about how he meant to use it. Midway through his rehearsal he stopped the cast and had them sit in a circle on the floor. He handed the bean bag to the person who had the first line in the scene, with these instructions: "As you deliver the *cue* words which prompt the response from the next character, throw the bean bag to that character. Now, realize that the impetus for the next speech may *not* necessarily be the last word of your line—so don't wait for that to throw the bag; throw it at the point in your speech which *begins* the impulse to respond." The scene started, and in moments, as it was a lively scene, the bag was flying across the circle with amazing speed as each actor followed the pattern of throwing-catching-throwing that the director had suggested.

After a few minutes of this, he stopped the actors and asked what they had learned by the exercise. Enthusiastically, they expressed their new understanding of interaction and pacing of a scene, which the bean bag had graphically demonstrated. "Now," he said, "I want that same feeling of throwing the bag and catching the bag as we play the scene on our feet." They rose and played the scene with a new awareness of the tempo and the interaction, which they had only vaguely realized before the bean bag exercise.

1

Struck as I was by the novelty of this approach and its apparent success, I tried the trick later while rehearsing a short, fast-moving scene from *The Rivals*. I gave my cast essentially the same exercise with the bean bag and was pleasantly rewarded with the same increase of awareness of actor interaction.

I mention this episode in detail because I think it illustrates two points to be made about this new edition of *Creative Dramatics for Children*. First, "creativity" in dramatics is not limited for playwrights and actors but infuses every aspect of production—directing, scene designing, lighting, costuming, props, publicity—and teaching. Nor is it limited to any single phase of a theatre person's life, amateur, student, or professional. It is an on-going process. Mrs. Durland is interested in introducing children to this kind of creativity as experiences and attitudes that will color their entire future lives.

Second, every director—and teacher—constantly experiments to find workable techniques. Over the years he collects a useful bag of tricks which can be used to advantage over and over again. This book is full of such techniques which the author has discovered through her own experience as a director of children's dramatics. Many of them will be of great value to the novice director, not only in realization of the ultimate performance but in the day-to-day avoidance of the unforeseen pitfalls which beset the beginner.

Creative Dramatics for Children was first published in 1952. The last copies of its fifth printing were sold out about two years ago. At that time it was felt that perhaps the book had lived out its life—was beginning to show its age in a few places, and could quietly be retired. But it had established itself as something of a classic in its field and orders and inquiries continued to arrive at the publisher's office—from teachers, education departments, day care center workers, theatre people. Far from being a past interest, creative dramatics—all creative work with children—was abounding in classroom and playground, summer camp and Sunday School.

So a new edition was considered. But was a complete revision really necessary? A new bibliography, certainly. And some updating of certain references: Do children nowadays know such stories as "Raggy Lug" and "Epaminandas"? In the description of plotless material (pages 27-28), how many of today's children have ridden on a streetcar? Or would know about a "late arrival at the opera"? The basic philosophy and techniques of Mrs. Durland's approach, however, are as timeless as a child's world may be transitory. One of her basic tenets is to seek experiences from the children's own lives, and a book like this can only suggest where to look, not what to find. On further thought, therefore, it was decided to reissue the book with a minimum of change, on the theory that a good theatre person does not rewrite or redirect a play in the middle of a long and successful run.

Perhaps because of its title, the first edition of this book found its greatest audience among teachers working with children in the early grades, and certainly a major portion of the book is addressed to their needs. But it has much to say to those working with older children, and even to me

3

working on the college-age level. Chapter Six on Creative Directing, in dealing with productions of already written plays, contains ideas as useful to the director of *Hamlet* as to the director of *Winnie the Pooh.* At all levels, the teacher's and director's functions is to draw out the creative potential of the actor he is working with—child or adult.

I want to emphasize, however, the subtle but essential distinction between creative dramatics and children's theatre; it is necessary that the teacher recognize them as different, if often interrelated, activities. Public performance may be a legitimate end goal of a children's dramatics program; children may want the acclaim of peers and parents, and the experience can be a good one. But the basic goal of creative dramatics is the child's growth and enjoyment of the creative *process.* That is the only aim. Children's theatre, on the other hand, is aimed at the audience from the beginning and that influences the preparation and rehearsal process. As with everything else in this book, the emphasis should remain on developing the child's values.

Certainly one of the most treasured ideas in the legacy left us by Stanislavsky is the notion that the creative spirit can thrive only in an atmosphere of harmony, freedom, mutual affection, and—yes, even love. Mrs. Durland's approach to creative dramatics never violates the child's need to create by authoritative imposition of the director's own creative impulse on that of the child. The child is encouraged, rather, to stretch (and strengthen) his own creativity by empathic identification of himself, as an actor, with the personality and desires of the character—a basically sound approach to acting at any level. Then, wisely, Mrs. Durland

4

goes beyond this first step and demonstrates to the beginning director—and thus to the actor—that a "character" is more than the simple behaviorism of the performer. She stresses that the actor should always ask himself what *this character* in *this situation* might do, and not exclusively what *the actor* would do in real life. Thus the basic steps in valid character analysis are made an inherent part of the rehearsal process, and the child is encouraged to imagine—and thus to create dramatically. And after all, what else is creative dramatics than this?

JIM BOB STEPHENSON
Kent State University

Foreword

"Creative Dramatics" is a manual for teacher, leaders and mothers. The purpose is twofold: To present a working method that is clear, concise and interesting; also to present the thought that all creative teaching is merely bringing the child to the threshold of his own mind. This book has grown out of ten years' experience as teacher of, and researcher in, creative living, with dramatics as the medium of expression. The educational and philosophical implications of the word "creative" are significant in the realm of dramatics, perhaps more than in any other form of teaching today, because in dramatic experience there is a unique opportunity for creative living; it is a slice of life.

The suggestion that the material gathered together should be put in book form came from teachers taking my course in "Creative Dramatics" offered by the University of California Extension Division.

This book, however, does not limit itself to an analysis of methods of teaching. Rather I have attempted to make clear that the basis of creative teaching of dramatics is much more complex than the art of play-acting. Rather, that it is a dramatic experience in creative group activity of profound significance to the development of character and personality. For this conception of creative teaching I wish to thank specifically: Miss Neva Boyd, of the Sociology Department of Northwestern University, whose unique contributions in the field of group activities need

7

no further mention; Mrs. Charlotte Chorpenning, of the Children's Theatre at Goodman's Theatre, Chicago; Miss Louise Guernsey, whose creative art work has been a source of joy; and Miss Maren Elwood, whose creative approach to writing has been a further delight.

The subject of creative dramatics for children has been in so experimental a stage that very little is to be found written; especially for the inexperienced worker; however, the educational trends are so definitely towards the creative that dramatics is becoming a part of regular classroom activities. The knowledge of how to do this creative work has not kept step with the demand for the work itself. The teacher asked to conduct such work frequently has had neither practical nor theoretical experience, hence has no resources to meet the need. She blunders on, unhappy in a field that should be fertile. For this reason I believe a practical manual has a very definite place and will be of wide interest to both teachers and laymen.

My idea is to present my material in such a manner that it will be acceptable—not only to teachers—but also to playground workers, camp directors, mothers, and all others who recognize the educational value, not only of dramatics as one art form, but of creative thinking for children. I go so far as to believe that mothers of young children may apply advantageously the philosophy of creative dramatics to their relationship with their own children in the home. As a mother I have found this creative philosophy a great help in understanding my own children. By such a creative approach to the child mind it has been possible to obtain an understanding of children that is objective and wise.

The underlying theme of all creative art is the same: to offer opportunity for richer living through an integrated personality. Dramatics offers an unusually fine field in this approach to creative living.

FRANCES CALDWELL DURLAND
Berkeley, California

Chapter One

Creative Dramatics

The educational trends of today are towards the creative in the teaching of art, music, drama or play. What is meant by "creative"? It may be defined by saying that to create is to bring to life or make something; to originate. Whatever form the art may assume it must come from within the person; from within the group. It is an expression of something evolved from within, not the imposition of a completed art form upon the individual or group. It is born from the union of technique and spontaneous expression.

To create dramatically is to build, through the imagination, a form or structure that we term a play. This play may be created from familiar life situations or from the classics of child literature. That is, the recognized dramatic structure of a play is the vehicle for creative effort on the part of the group. It is, however, flexible in the manner of its expression.

There is a definite technique of approach exactly as there is in any other art. This approach is to analyze step by step the meaning of creative dramatics and the application of the technique necessary to its success. The potentialities of dramatics as an educational force, as well as an art, are already recognized. Creative dramatics may be a vital power for the education both of mind and character. Character is created; dramatics can be a cornerstone of that building.

Our great difficulty lies, not in lack of recognition of the value of creative dramatics for children, but in the vagueness existing in the minds of dramatically untrained teachers as to how to obtain effective results. This is due to the fact that, comparatively speaking, creative dramatics is a new field of experiment. A shift in emphasis has come into being.

The emphasis in the past was upon the production in group dramatics; upon elocution in the individual performance. Drama was first of all for the stage; for actors, actresses and artists. The rest participated vicariously as the audience. Colleges were the first to adventure into the histrionic arts; usually in one or two Shakespearian presentations yearly. Now almost all colleges have a well-equipped dramatics department. Some have a school of the theatre, professional in its scope; high schools followed more slowly, but many of them today have excellent departments. The Little Theatre movement needs no discussion. Its most outstanding contribution perhaps has been to prove that in most of us there is a dramatic sense from which we derive creative satisfaction. It is one of the outstanding sources of leisure-time enjoyment today.

Last of all was the sudden awakening to the possibilities of creative dramatics for children. Their inherent sense of make-believe, which is the essence of drama, was recognized as an excellent vehicle of learning.

The educational awakening as to the possibilities of creative dramatics for the child ended, to a large extent,

11

the era of artificiality in dramatics for children. Previous to that time drama was for the talented few; with emphasis upon spectacular stage effects, and an eye on applause and the box office. Attractive and gifted children were exploited that the "show" might be an artistic success. No consideration was given to the effect upon the character of the children so exploited or upon those left out. Elocution was even more detrimental since it was not only artificial but also singled out one child for attention.

Even today, dramatics often has as its sole objective a spectacular performance that has nothing of the creative about it. Little or no thought is given to the social values. The performance is the product, not of the children's creative development, but of the art ideal of the director. Plays, costumes, and stage effects as well as interpretation of lines are the choice of the teacher. They are imposed upon the group; the rehearsals are drill, not education. How valuable the experience is will depend upon the gifts of the leader. There is, of course, a place for the more formal dramatics but it should not displace the more creative work, which is essentially educational.

The shortcomings of this formal type of dramatics—especially for young children—are obvious: the excitement of over-stimulation, unhealthy competition, and the all-too-frequent artificiality both of line and gesture. These plays are in no sense a product of the child mind. The relation between formal dramatics and original plays lies in the inherent dramatic feeling that is latent in all of us. Dramatics of the older type uses only the talented. Creative dramatics utilizes this universal dramatic feeling

12

as a means of education, and it fosters the happiness that is the result of establishing a creative emotional outlet for the individual.

The evolution from formal to informal came through the gradual recognition of the potentialities of creative dramatics for all children. The newer educational methods of creative emphasis opened up further interest. The change from formal education to the project method needs no discussion. We need only point out that when the child's natural talents for make-believe and drama received full recognition as a tool for education, creative dramatics, as such, won a place for itself, not as an art, but as a means of presenting study material; and also as one of the finest expressions of social experience.

Creative dramatics is an expression of the newer educational ideas of today. It has only two serious handicaps—except for the untrained public which wants to see cute children in cunning plays—(1) the lack of understanding of the possibilities of creative effort, and (2) the lack of training in the knowledge of how to effect the desired artistic results. Both of these are due solely to the teacher's lack of training.

There seems to be a keen interest in creative plays in school and recreation centers. But there seems, also, to be a definite lack of knowledge as to just what a creative play is, and how one obtains such knowledge; often there is a lack of clearness as to what is the fundamental difference between a creative play and one that is not. One of the greatest handicaps found by groups of teachers in successive classes of study in this subject proved to be the

13

demands made upon them to produce a creative play within a certain time limit. That this is a very difficult thing to do is understood by the teacher, but frequently not by the supervisor or principal.

Another fallacy seems to be that any teacher can produce creative plays. It is true that a very imaginative and creative-minded teacher may produce an acceptable effort. She could, however, do so with much more happiness, both for herself and the children, with a knowledge of technique. One is not expected to teach reading without a thorough knowledge of method; there is a method of attack in producing creative plays that are artistically satisfactory.

There are fundamental problems that immediately confront the teacher: a choice of material, disciplinary problems related to the production, behavior and psychological factors, and short cuts to successful performance. All these are not just classroom problems but change with the dramatic adventure. What is the teacher to do in the face of a specific situation? Where may she obtain quickly the necessary answer to her problem? The plays presented in outline form in this manual have been given by children creatively. They offer suggestions for like situations.

It is significant that the first general use of this natural flair for dramatic play, on the part of the child, came from the shift in emphasis in educational trends. Social studies were vitalized by putting information gathered by the group into play form. Material thus gathered became more appealing to the mind and imagination and therefore, was more readily retained in the mind. However, these playforms, while presenting fact material more vitally to the child, are not truly dramatic. The end in view is the knowledge to be gained, whereas a true play is a story in action.

Therefore the procedure in the mind of the director has as its goal an awakening perception of the drama of life. The teacher's object is far more comprehensive than to build dialogue around an informative theme; her function is to take a slice out of life and, by imaginative treatment, to make of it a reality for her children. Creative dramatics is such a powerful force for life development that understanding of its technique is repaid in spiritual coin. It is one of the finest tools by which a group may be welded together into greater sympathy and understanding. Group experience of the highest order is one of the byproducts. Interest, enthusiasm and joy are shared alike as well as responsibility and hard work.

If the citizen of today needs mental poise and a broader vision, it is not too much to say that he may make a real beginning through creative dramatics. The child is bringing to life, through his individual and group efforts, a living play, one on his own emotional level, portraying life and people as he sees and feels them. It might be said, in passing, that a dislike for dramatics is often a result of stilted, stiff and uninteresting so-called creative play. There must be a clear understanding as to where dramatized material leaves off and an action play begins. What are the differences? How may project material be made dramatic? And why should it be dramatic?

One of the first questions asked by teachers is why attempt to create a play when it is much easier to direct a play already written. The answer is largely in the dearth of material. Also, even when there is delightful material it is often unsuitable. Generally speaking, artistic plays written for children are not written with the child mind in view. They are not in his diction or expressive of his feelings. We, as adults, can rarely place ourselves in the imagination of the child. His thought processes differ; his sense of humor is not ours, and his perceptions leave us upon another level. How can we use our superior knowledge to bring into play his natural endowment?

In a play that is already written, the child learns from memory and at the dictation of another. It is true that in his first crude efforts at building his own play, the diction may not be as finished as in that of a play written for his entertainment by an adult. But if he must find the words with which to clothe his thoughts and feelings, in the long run he will build up better speech. He learns very little, if anything, of dramatic form through drill in even a lovely play, although his sense of beauty may be stirred. But when by means of class discussion he learns the stuff of which a play is made—to sense drama; to help build a structure with a beginning, middle and end; to create suspense and exciting moments—he carries this feeling for drama on to development. Last, and by no means least, in the creative play each child has equal opportunity since the goal is not production, but education of the individual. The production is his; he is a part of the group that brings life to this play. He may only be the one who rings down the curtain, but he is an important cog in the group exercise. He comes out of the experience a richer and happier personality. He has learned to think and act creatively; he has learned the great sociological lesson of cooperation.

This cooperation is the basis of the group idea. A group is more than a collection of people working together. It is a process of integration within the people in a new combination of thoughts. It is an important essential in the development or enrichment of both the individual and the group since it comes not from the imposition of ideas by the leader, but out of mutual discussion. A group idea becomes larger than any concept that one individual may hold because it is the result of the union of minds. It can never develop in any situation where discussion is not an integral part of the set-up. You may take a so-called group and by presentation of your material have it accepted. But you have lost thereby the deeper value of growth which is the outcome of mind acting upon mind.

Suggested reading:

Austin, Mary. *Every Man's Genius*. Indianapolis: The Bobbs Merrill Co., 1925.

Boyd, Neva. *Social Life For The Group*. Bulletin, V. 1, No. 1. Northwestern University, Univ. College., Div. of Social Work.

Mursell. *Using Your Mind Effectively*. New York: McGraw-Hill, 1951.

Creative Dramatics for Children

Chapter I: *Questions for Student Teachers*

1. In what specific ways can you enlarge your own concept of the deeper meanings in the word "creative"?

2. How can you determine whether your "creative" play is becoming an exhibition instead of a functioning group?

3. When first considering your class, what measuring rod can you use to discover the relative creative freedom of the group?

4. If you are an inexperienced teacher, about to adventure into a creative drama with your group, what would be your first steps?

5. Outline in your own mind the essential differences between the values, both for yourself and the children, of the created play and the formulated play.

Chapter I: *Summary*

1. To create is to: bring to life or to make; to originate. It is the underlying philosophy, not only of creative dramatics, but of all art, of all highly evolved living.

2. Creative dramatics as an educational force is a corner stone of character building.

3. A discussion of formal dramatics and creative dramatics must reveal the comparative value of the two as educational forces.

4. A brief analysis of what constitutes a group.

18

Source Material for Creative Dramatics

Material that lends itself to creative drama may be drawn from the following sources:

1. Myths
2. Folklore
3. Fairy Tales
4. Historical Material
5. Nature
6. Animal Stories
7. Life

One of the essential ingredients for success lies in the choice of material. Not all stories or bits of drama from life lend themselves equally well to creative drama. Material to be used for a play must have action. The story or original form must lend itself to simple sequences, one succeeding the other towards a climax; or as children say to the most "exciting" moment. In addition to action it should have some significance. Many of the difficulties that teachers meet with are due to the fact that a story or historical subject is often too lacking in movement and is uninteresting as well. Hence in a very brief time the children have exhausted its possibilities, become bored, restless and tend to repeat themselves. The teacher or director concludes from one or two such performances

19

that there is no value in creative dramatics and gives up the experiment. The failure lies, not in creative dramatics, or the children, but in the teacher's choice of subjects.

The significance of the material chosen may lie in its literary value, its beauty of thought and conception, in the educational merits derived from the information. It may be that it gives emotional expression and poise, or it may be a source of delightful pleasure in itself. It is far easier for a beginner to obtain satisfactory results from a well-chosen story, especially from folklore and fairy tale material, than to originate a play from life problems. This is because a great many of these stories have an excellent skeleton upon which to build. They are simple, direct and usually contain a core of truth easily recognized by children. They are easier to build into the structure of a play since the fundamentals are already present. They are in themselves vital.

Other things to be considered in selection of material are its possibilities of characterization. Little children and beginners in the creative art need sharply defined characters. They will build up the finer points of characterization through experience but a story of commonplace people doing commonplace things is not stimulating, either to mind or emotion. Since dialogue is the outgrowth of character and motivation it should be interesting.

On the other hand many stories, myths, and incidents lend themselves to simple story-playing but not to dramatization in its more formal sense. This manual does not aim to take up the finer points of play-writing, an art in itself, but to make clear the fundamentals necessary for successful creative activity. However, there are three successive steps to be taken up:

1. Story telling
2. Story playing
3. The more formal dramatization that must also be flexible and fluid.

If the objective is a brief experiment in classroom activities that include story-playing, one does not need to consider the limitations of a stage; the unities need not be so strictly adhered to, although if interest is not sustained the teacher is setting a future problem for herself.

Finally then, one must select material that has action, significance and lends itself to sustained interest.

Another consideration is that of age suitability. The younger the child the more essential is wise choice in material. The little child is limited in his characterization by his own immaturity of conception; hence action plays a great part. He feels, sees and thinks in action; he has no reflective development. His story action material must not be too complicated but it must be of interest. As the maturity increases the choice may be more comprehensive. Fairy tales find a place in the imagination of all children. Difference in the degree of elaboration of setting and dialogue would be the essential changes.

When historical material is selected, whether the end is assimilation of knowledge or a period play, the subject-matter should be dramatic. If the incident itself is not significant, it must be built up by added complications, real or imaginary. This may be accomplished in a fascinating manner when both the leader and group are adept at creative playing. The same is true of the play evolved from life situations. The difficulty with so many plays of this type is their lack of motivation, characterizations and interesting dialogue. One must remember that although the results of the first efforts may be crude, they will later acquire polish. All the first efforts should be simple. Work with a simple theme, short and vivid. Allow free play with such material until the children are mentally prepared for the more expansive type of dramatization.

Call the work creative but do not confuse it with a play. It is usually a series of episodes put together for the purpose of presenting a program before the school, class, or playground. Nevertheless it is a first step and is very valuable as such.

Suggested material:

Wee Willie Winkie	Henny Penny
Georgie Porgy	Three Billy Goats Gruff
Old Mother Hubbard	The Three Little Kittens
Simple Simon	Why the Evergreen Tree
Mulberry Bush	Keeps Its Leaves
Tom, Tom the Piper's Son	Epaminandas
Old King Cole	Little Red Hen and the Grain
The Knave of Hearts	of Wheat
Jack and Jill	Ginger Bread Boy
Three Bears	Peter Pan
Three Little Pigs	Cinderella
Nature Tales	Tar Baby
Raggy Lug	Jack and the Bean Stalk
The Pig Brother	Sleeping Beauty

22

Source Material

A further bibliography will be found in the appendix.

Chapter II: *Questions*

1. Can you clearly analyze and outline in your own mind why some otherwise excellent material is unsuitable for a play?

Chapter II: *Summary*

1. Stories adaptable for dramatic plays must have: action and significance.

2. Consideration of the educational objective in the choice of material. Is it the dissemination of facts? Or is it an art form?

3. Suggested stories suitable for dramatization.

Chapter Three

Technique of the Story Drama

For technical reasons the plans may be divided into three parts:

1. The study of stories
2. Story playing
3. Story drama, the structural art form of creative plays.

These will be taken up, step by step, and the relation between them shown. To be creative, dramatics must be approached with the awareness that time is essential for any creative effort. Educational results cannot be obtained under the pressure of time; if the teacher becomes impatient and forces the flower it will bloom too soon only to die. Far better take the simplest possible form and develop it to the ultimate, than to fail in one's first creative efforts. Nor can the teacher assume that the stiff and indifferent product resulting from a few hours of play is a truly creative expression of her group.

The teacher must bear in mind two facts (we are assuming that both she and her group are more or less new at this field of experiment): she must herself understand how to learn to create; she must inspire and free her group of children in the creative realm.

Far from being a dull or stupid form of activity with children, it may be the source of great spiritual uplift.

No special dramatic gift is needed either by the teacher or the children. However, there must be a sensitivity and perception of values and the ability to draw forth from even the most inhibited small being some creative feeling. What could be more inspirational than to be able to build a living emotional freedom for little children? Is there anything more exciting for the leader of children than to watch a progressive personality development? And to know that the means of this awakening lies within the grasp of the teacher in her knowledge of creative play? Not only does the creative gift offer life to those children who participate in the unfolding of the story, but the teacher shares in this recreation.

The teacher must constantly bear in mind that group activity is the source of vitality to her and her children. Group activity is the functioning of collective ideas in an integrated manner. That is, there is an interaction of minds and emotions *out of which grows* the creative whole. It cannot be imposed; it must be a result.

It is a most interesting fact that those who do creative work draw deeply upon some inner reservoir of life that again and again fills them anew mentally and spiritually. If you come away tired and nervous from the hours of work with your group, you have not tapped, within yourself, or in them, that vast storehouse of power that lies within each of us. However perfect, from the standpoint of technique, the rehearsal may have been, you have nevertheless failed in the creative. To do really creative work means to escape fatigue into a realm of illusion and power. When you come to a rehearsal weary, and go away renewed, then you have succeeded in being creative. You have tapped group energy.

If the pressure of time is used to force the growth, the finer aspects of creative work will be lost. Far better, if the demand is made to have a play ready at a certain date, either to select a play already written, or have a creative program of material—not dramatic in form.

Why is time essential? Let us define "creative." To create is to bring to life, to build, or to bring into being. We have already discussed the importance of our choice of material to the success or failure of our final dramatic adventure (Chapter II). How do we create? *Through the use of the imagination.*

A play sets forth in art form lives and characters other than our own. A play must have action, suspense, climax, dialogue, characterization, and some degree of unity. Obviously we cannot hope to build such a structure without some experience on the part of ourselves and our co-operating group. This preliminary experience is sought through imaginative participation in story-playing. It is common to all life; it is the natural approach of a child to life; even adults dramatize although it is called by another name.

Emphasis is not to be upon the production as such, but rather, upon the growth that comes from within. This growth will come gradually, over a period of time. As the teacher herself grows in understanding and skill, improvement will come. The awakening within the group will express itself in greater spontaneity and joy.

It would seem, then, that one of the fundamentals of

creative dramatics is an understanding of imagination and its function. It is readily accepted that all children are not equally gifted or developed in this quality. One of the first tasks then is to awaken imagination. How is this to be done? And what is imagination?

Imagination is the quality of mind and spirit that enables one to understand experiences beyond his own. They may be of the environment or of the spirit or emotions. This capacity to imagine enriches not only one's own life, but that of others. The immediate problem is to find the relationship between the imagination and the natural dramatic instinct of the child. Before taking this up in detail, it might be well to enlarge upon the importance of imagination. Most of us reach out through our reading, travel and human experience to the realm of others. The capacity for living is greatly increased as this ability to understand the lives of others develops. Children often have an inherent quality of imagination or make-believe that is allowed to die, or at best is never developed. The unhappy results of these lacks are evident in world and civic affairs of today.

In creative dramatics the teacher acts as the torch to light the flame of imagination. She is not giving plays only—she is giving life to the soul—the current of lives may well be changed by her inspiration. Therefore no effort should be spared to allow this great creative force to grow, to come into being.

One of the most elementary types of creative play is the use of plotless material. Select the incidents out of life with which the group are familiar but that have possibilities of action. Allow them to act these out. One may term this sort of acting "limbering up." Such material is valuable in that usually the entire group may be used once; thus eliminating one of the arch enemies—self-consciousness. One half the group acts while the other half is the audience. Then reverse the group procedure.

Such incidents as the following are suggested:

1. A group going on a street car to the beach.
2. A bargain counter.
3. A family automobile ride.
4. Riding the ponies at the park.
5. Swimming in cold water.
6. A group of brownies or elves.
7. Buying shoes or hats.
8. At a movie.
9. For older children the portrayal of emotional feeling such as pride, joy, anger, in pantomime.
10. Late arrival at the opera.

The ingenuity of the teacher and the group can supply endless material. The objectives of the use of this sort of play are:

1. As stated above—to allow for group action when neither teacher nor group have had much experience in creative play.

2. To arouse interest in creative play.

3. To permit the development of a more spontaneous state of mind in the group.

4. To utilize material that lends itself to only a few rehearsals until the group is ready for more sustained effort.

28

It is well, perhaps, at this point to state again that this should be in the nature of play, but has no structural form. The purpose is entirely that of a pleasurable exercise. It may be made more elaborate by a study of individual characterization. I have found this an excellent way in which to stimulate mental activity, as well as observation. We would discuss the traits that are to be noticed in people, and then portray them. For example, if a scene is selected from a street car we assign to each player entering the car a dominant trait—pride, insolence, happiness, grouchiness, so on throughout the list of human attributes. The audience is part of the game and guesses what sort of person is before them. If dialogue is included we discuss "how such a person would talk."

Even such simple and elementary dramatized play may be developed into amusing and vital sketches. There should be no idea of presenting a play at this period of study. The emphasis is placed entirely upon the interest in developing specific detail. When it will be played out—as it will be in a few rehearsals—go on to a more advanced theme.

What part does the teacher play in this dramatization? Since her part remains the same whether the objective is story-playing, drama, or this more simple play we may well go into more detail at this time. She is the leader, not the dictator. In the more formal type of dramatics, especially a few years ago, her duties were to plan and put into execution every detail. The amount of creative freedom permitted to the participants was decided entirely by her temperament. Usually, for the sake of an artistic production, the whole play was an expression of her artistic conception.

The role of the teacher, or director, in creative drama is exactly the opposite. She leads, or draws out of her group by means of skillful suggestions and questions the latent capacity in individual and group. In so far as possible she allows the children to proceed without interruption. The creative flow is stopped as readily by too much interference as by a failure to perceive when suggestions are needed. I will take this up in greater detail soon. Generally speaking, however, the time for new suggestion or group discussion is when the children have ceased to create and imitate that which has already been developed. In the first attempts of any group accustomed to having been told just what to do, and when to do it, in dramatics or elsewhere, there are going to be static moments. Your function, as the teacher, is to throw the discussion back to the group. Thus they are stimulated. The less the group has been permitted to act on their own, the more difficult and slow will the results be—and the less worthwhile.

STORY-TELLING

Story-telling is the fundamental step in dramatic art for children. It is the means by which the child first participates imaginatively in the emotions and experiences of others.

What is the function of the story? It is not only to arouse interest in literature. Story-telling is one of the oldest and most beloved of the arts; out of its legends

have come our great children's classics. All children love
a story. It is the open sesame to the heart of a child. How
then may we as teachers make use of this love in our
creative field?

Let us first discuss reading the story versus telling it.
There are, of course, times when the teacher must read
stories rather than tell them; this is true especially of long
and complicated stories. The demands upon her time may
be such that proper learning of the story is out of the
question; or she may wish to retain the diction in its
beauty and perfection. Usually, however, the teacher or
the leader who resorts to reading rather than telling the
story loses a certain rapport with the group. When the
story is read the book comes between the reader and the
group; there is a fine shade of unity destroyed. On the
other hand when the story is *told*, the teacher uses her
eyes, body and mood to make the story live; her audience
is at one with her and the character she portrays.

To prove the truth of this statement one need only
to take any slightly disorganized group of children and
try both methods. I have had many story hours for settlement children. In almost none of them would it have
been possible to read from a book and keep their attention. Any one of the same stories could be told to the
group and hold them spell-bound; you cannot *read* to
the one or two disturbing children but you can *tell* the
story to the rebels and gradually draw them into the
magic circle.

Let us assume now that you, a teacher, wish to build
plans for a year of creative dramatics. For the sake of

clearness we will consider that you are embarking upon a new adventure. How shall you start?

You will first of all select a story. Your age-group will determine its nature to some extent. The story must be interesting. It must have significance. You may draw upon fairy tales with their kinship to the past; with their portrayal of life truths taught through imagery. Or perhaps you prefer a nonsense tale, with its sense of humor that may so aptly give the necessary sense of proportion in life. Your choice may be from nature, history, sociology, or other sources. Tell several stories to the group and let them select for dramatization the one they like best.

There is a technique to making story telling easier also. Never tell a story unless you *know* it. To learn it do not memorize it word for word. Proceed in the following fashion:

1. Memorize the skeleton of the story.
2. Make it a personal experience—catch the atmosphere.
3. Have each picture in it clearly visualized.
4. Memorize the sequence of the scenes.
5. Avoid hesitancy and self-interruption.
6. Keep the literary style of the author but do not memorize the material.

A short cut for accomplishing this is to use outlines. Tell the story to yourself, or any one else who will lend an ear, until it flows freely. After you have gone over this laboriously a few times, it will, like other creative efforts, flow with more ease.

Selecting and learning your story is the first step to be accomplished. Now we shall consider the next step that takes place: to be assured of building the proper dramatic effect in them, you must arrange your audience. The most satisfactory way is to place them in a semicircle, facing you. This enables the teacher to easily catch the eye of each listener. The manner of telling may be happily worked out as follows:

1. Tell the story very directly and with vitality.
2. Tell the story simply.
3. Tell it only as dramatically as the story permits.
   Do not make yourself stand out.

When the story has been told, with the idea in mind that it may be utilized as a story-play, the first step is completed. At this point a story may be discussed by the group. It should bring up the following points:

1. Meaning of the story?
2. Why it is interesting?
3. What are the outstanding crises in the story?

The next and last step in preparation for story-playing is again to tell the story. The purpose of this is to make it a living experience for both the group and the teacher. Now the story is ready to be transferred into action.

STORY-PLAYING

Again let us stress the fact that the time element must be given full recognition. The teacher and group are setting forth together upon a creative enterprise, away from imitation towards creation and free energy. You—as the leader—are opening up vistas of life and a truer appreciation, not only of drama, but of life itself. The emphasis has shifted from the finished product to the development of the producers. The entire study is a group enterprise, social as well as creative.

If the story has been wisely chosen—with action and significance—your rehearsal material should grow each day for a period of weeks, or even months. If it is possible to give one hour daily, such a story as "Snow White and the Seven Dwarfs" should be allowed to develop for at least a month. It will, if properly done, grow creatively, losing nothing in vitality and interest, for even a longer period. If it does not, there is something wrong with your technique. This period does not include the transition period to the drama form. It may, in an advanced group, but we are assuming that you are beginners. If the group comes only once a week there is the more difficult problem of sustained interest and the development period will take far longer. Enthusiasm and creative flow diminish between rehearsals.

I have already pointed out that the teacher's place is that of a more or less silent partner. The great temptations to an inexperienced creative director are:

1. The desire to hurry.
2. To step into a difficult situation and to point out *what* to do and *how* to do it.
3. To fail to keep one's own creative alertness and hence allow the group to become bored.
4. To drill, rather than create.

The desire to hurry is due to the feeling of pressure in getting things accomplished; to the awkwardness of beginners; and to the teacher's own unwillingness truly to complete the experiment. To be successful one must go all the way. Otherwise the true joy of creative art is not experienced.

What are the objectives of the leader? Broadly speaking they are: to obtain creative freedom, dramatic appreciation of situations, resourcefulness and initiative in the group.

Play the story without interruption the first few times. The first and most discouraging problem that appears is that most of the children are inhibited, emotionally and physically. The story has been told. Now let us go back and consider the technique, step by step.

You ask the class, "Let us play this story out. How many would like to do so?" The response is most enthusiastic. Then allow each child to choose the character he would like to interpret. At this point we will give a few words to discussing casting. The first half a dozen rehearsals or playing periods, there should be several casts. Not only should there be several casts but the Queen should become the Lady-in-Waiting and so on. The reason for this shifting is obvious. You are offering creative opportunity to all, not to just the talented or aggressive child. The shy child who will not ask for a part, but shows her longing indirectly, must become a part of the enterprise. The whole affair is a group enterprise in which every child shall participate either actively or imaginatively.

The teacher will find that changing the cast is one of her best devices for keeping alive class interest. By interchange, each child continues to feel himself a part of the creative whole. Not only that, but you, as teacher, will find a sense of joy in the unfoldment of the timid or less brilliant child through the expansion of self expression. To create even a few sentences in a play is more of a spiritual and mental and emotional triumph for such a child, then to memorize, under the direction of another, a longer part. I recall so well one little Polish child, at Hull House nursery school, who had been in a play for some time. Her background was pitiful. Nothing in it at all of loveliness. After working with her for several months, we gave the play; her contribution was about six lines. Afterwards the little thing came up to me and timidly took my hand. "Teacher, I loved the play. I'll be all lonely again now." She patted her costume of bright but inexpensive cloth, "It's so pretty."

That child had been lifted out of her sordid environment into the realm of imagination. Yet, had this not been creative work she could not possibly have been equal to portraying a part. The changing cast in itself gives confidence to the children because they know that other children will also take the parts. There is always the assurance that comes from knowing the whole, not only the part. Furthermore, it has its value for the too aggressive child since he does not gather for himself all the plums. For the teacher, it affords the opportunity to feel out for future productions the latent capacities of her group.

After several rehearsals have been played out in a very elementary form, with shifting casts, the next step may be taken. Already you will have had a few problems come up, such as: the children will give the story almost as it was read or told to them and there will be almost no originality. Do not be tempted because of this to assume that nothing will develop. *It has not been creative at all up to this point.* It has merely been an exercise in remembering and a way to stir up a desire to play.

The story is chosen; a tentative cast ready. What is now your procedure? You do not need any stage, nor any unity of time or place. Ask perhaps, "Where shall we have the house of the Queen? Where the house of the Dwarfs? And what shall be used as the mountains between the two?" In this way the entire room may be used freely.

The play is now started. And as we stated, the first reaction will be that of pure imitation or memory work. The children will most of them stand around and ask you—the teacher—what to do. They will have no freedom of action. This, largely, because of no experience in creative work. When you have changed casts several times and the play remains static, it is time for you to step in and bring it to life with well-directed questions. Think of your group as a cooperating social and artistic unit, with yourself as the leader. Ask one question that will start the creative feeling of the group. That question might be about one of the three following things (if using Snow White): what is an outstanding trait of the Queen? Have the whole group discuss the Queen until her outstanding characteristics are well understood. Next, how does the Queen show these character traits? And what effect do they have upon the other people in the story and why? These, of course, are only suggested questions. All leadership of creative work depends for its life upon the ability *to stir in others* those feelings, emotions, and ideas that build up the creative product.

Imagination is the spiritual quality that enables us to feel for others; to suffer with others, and to be happy with them. A play, finished or crude, must possess illusion. *Your greatest problem is to create imagination in the child.* Or at least to awaken it. This may only be done by enlarging the horizon of the child by greater experiences, emotional and mental. Merely permitting a group of children to go through a story, with no development on their part, does nothing for them creatively. However, the minute you and the class begin functioning as a social unit with an artistic aim, you are creating. That is the secret of keeping interest and inspiration growing. Each rehearsal should definitely close with a sense of enrichment, together with an elation anticipating the next. New movements should have grown out of the study of motives of the characters within the play; the body becomes the medium of a new personality and new dialogue grows out of a discussion of the characters and their function within the story. If this is done the only limit to the growth of the group lies in its mental capacity and in the creative richness of the leader. Such creative teaching truly leads a child to the threshold of his mind.

The first indications of imaginative fertility often confuse an inexperienced leader in this creative field. If you are using discussion and leading questions, pertinent to the story itself and *are not interfering too much* with the creative flow, there will begin to be, after about the first four rehearsals, an expansion in the use of material. You will find all sorts of irrelevant material appearing in your story. It may come out of familiar fairy tales, other stories, or from life situations. Do not, at first, make any effort to discard this subject-matter. Later you can show that it has no real relationship to the story. At the present your objective is to *free* the group, in so far as possible. Let the children offer all the material available and create dialogue around it. Thus you will get spontaneity. If, on the contrary, you interrupt, discard and correct, the very breath of life will be killed. The essence of creative drama is its childlike quality; its virtue lies in its fluid, changing growth. If the teacher tries to force the bloom the flower will not mature.

Child humor is another aspect that needs to be considered in the creative play. The sense of humor of a child differs from that of an adult. It is more primitive. He gets amusement out of that which seems crude to us, or humorless. However, unless the horseplay gets out of hand it is only a phase and may be ignored. If it tends to become too violent, curb it by showing that there is no relation between it and the story; that, in truth, it hinders or even blocks the development of the story.

It is remarkable how children may be taught to observe character and its workings. There is no limit to the fascination of discussion in this realm of the play, and it is highly valuable, not only as an exercise for creative play but as a training for the future. When a child is creating a character by means of the study of people—what they do, say and feel, he is expanding his spiritual understanding of life. Our limitations in understanding determine our capacity for our happiness.

One helpful way to get freedom of characterization is by the use of such questions as these: *How do people act* when they feel certain emotions? *What* makes them feel as they do? *How* do we motivate this when we are creating a play? It comes down to the *why* and *how* that children readily understand.

As the play develops, you must be re-creating yourself constantly. For if you—the leader—become indifferent, the play cannot stay alive. It will degenerate into drill, or imitation of itself, without vitality. When you have developed to their utmost all possibilities within the story, and have allowed each child to participate in the cast, and the interest is at a high pitch—then, and only then, are you ready to take up the fascinating task of story-drama.

We must not forget that we are striving for beauty constantly: beauty of words, ideas, and thoughts. We are seeking this beauty in the creative impulse. We are about to take the loose form of story-play, and of it make an art form, or drama. Our foundation in the weeks of free play has been sound. Now the torch of interest is lit; the children ready. That is the fundamental accomplishment of the weeks spent in creative play; although certain technical points may have also been covered such as: certain large movements of the story, a mild feeling for plot, and certainly dialogue.

Out of these weeks has come a sense of at-one-ness with your group that it is impossible to effect in any other way. You, as well as they, have stepped away from imitation towards the free energy derived from the creative world. In the next step you, the teacher, have the opportunity to build an appreciation of drama, an appreciation for situations that are fraught with life values, and to develop in the children the qualities of resourcefulness and ingenuity in dealing with them.

Immediately you will find yourself facing a different technique of procedure. There is a considerable difference in the detail of rehearsal and objective of story-play and story-drama. In the former, your objectives were to set the group free by means of creative *play*. Now you are about to use that creative force to construct an art form. At first, as has been pointed out, one does not curb the imagination as it expresses itself in many details that may be of no interest to the future audience. But imagination has served its purpose of limbering up. The group has begun to integrate within itself.

When you feel that the group is ready for the drama, present it to them as a dramatic experience, not as a dramatic production. A dramatic experience is one by which the individual and group are changed in patterns of thought—a rearrangement of the personality pattern. This does not mean that there is to be no directed effort towards the production, but it does mean that your real emphasis is still upon the creative flow. These are the steps to be taken:

1. The process of elimination of the uninteresting and irrelevant material.

2. The memorization of the skeleton of the story—this should be already clearly in mind. But if not, it must be discussed again and again since it is the foundation of the play that is to be given. It may be termed "Dramatic Line." It is the inner and underlying meaning of the play, around which everything else is built.

3. In the play there must be a beginning, a middle, and an end. All dialogue must further the plot, as well as delineate character and show the emotional state of the speaker.

4. Climax, characterization, conflict and dialogue, must be motivated and clearly understood. I think that with young children the words, "the most exciting point in the play" are better understood than the term "climax."

5. The following points will be kept well in mind: proportion, unity, art, beauty of thought and diction and dramatic line.

6. The best means of keeping within the story. Now let us start out in some such fashion as this: "Children, we have been playing this story quite a while, how would you like to make a real play of it?" Undoubtedly there will be a delightful and happy response to this question. All children love a play. However, children who have once become free in creative play never again are satisfied with more formal drama—not until about high-school age when the point of view changes. If they have had the creative experience before that time, they bring a greater spontaneity to the written play—and creative

coaching may be carried over into the play direction itself.

If possible, do not set a date for your play until it is just about ready. The feeling of working under time pressure is detrimental to the more creative aspects of the work. There are occasions, of course, when the teacher must meet the demands of a definite date. That is one of the advantages in keeping some creative work going during the entire school year. Then when the sudden demand comes it is quite possible to meet it without pressure.

The next step now is to cast. I am assuming that during the free-play period there has been a changing cast. The most satisfactory way, I believe for the final choice, is to allow the class to select the cast, drawing upon their experience of the past few weeks. Here again you will get your best results by having it clearly understood that the cast is interchangeable at any time.

The reasons for this are obvious: interest is kept alive through a bit of healthy competition; also, there is a psychological factor that deserves consideration; that is, the effect of one personality upon another. The impact of personality is sure to have its creative effect. Children are as much people in this respect as any adult. Therefore, it is quite possible for two children, who are playing opposite to each other to have an adverse effect on each other. One child may overpower a more timid but equally gifted child; or neither may draw the other out; or both may so stimulate each other that the rest of the cast cannot create at all. If you bear constantly in mind that the whole desire is not to produce an artistic result only, but is to encourage a group of artistic and social-minded children, it will be seen why the *individual development* of each child must ever be in mind.

Elimination of unnecessary material that the children have built up in the form of dialogue is the next step. *Only that which pertains to the actual building up of the story must be retained*. It does not follow, however, that what is left, after a study of what is important and what is not, will have no new dialogue added. On the contrary, most of your building is ahead of you—as you know, limbering up was just a part of the whole.

One of the first questions then is, "How can any particular bit of dialogue that is delightful in its imaginative expression be retained?" It can be, but must be done subtly. You cannot attempt to have it presented in just the same words. However, you can call attention to the fact that the idea is charming and suitable to the play; and suggest that it be incorporated into the play since it so well expresses the feelings of the character portrayed. In this case show by discussion with the group why and how this bit of dialogue is suitable to the play. Do not ever put the words of the character into the mouths of your children. Allow them, by means of detailed discussion, to decide this for themselves. When the play seems to be at a creative standstill it is only an indication to you, as the leader, that you are either dictating too much, or you are failing to put the points to be considered under discussion with the group. If there seems to be a lack of imagination upon the part of the Queen in the story of

Snow White and the Dwarfs, the following are some of the questions that the class may take up to again start their imaginations:

1. What are some of the attributes of a Queen?

2. How can these be expressed?

3. What in the story makes this particular Queen have the emotion that is hers?

4. How can this be shown?

5. What relation to the story as a whole does this emotion or act have?

6. How does her jealousy affect her deeds and words in regard to others? Her jealousy *motivates* the action of Snow White. Out of the conflicts between her emotions and the loveliness of Snow White emerges the plot, step by step.

This may be done with every character. The teachers in my classes seemed, on the whole to have more difficulty with dialogue than with characterization. The two are a part of a whole. Character determines our acts, and our speech. Motives are a part of character. If you make clear to your class that what the character says is determined by what he is like (feels, thinks and, as a result, does) it will be much simpler. Help the children to see *cause* and *effect* in the play. There must be logic in the train of events, and logic in character action. Think of your play in terms of natural experiences of the unfoldment of the characters. Would the character speak thus, or act so? And bear in mind constantly that drama lies in clash—of action, character, emotion, will, and story. Therein lies the fault in many so-called plays, there is no drama—they are a collection of incidents strung together by words—and hence are not capable of being creatively developed.

Dialogue determines, more than any one other element, the interest of your group, and the audience, in the play. Therefore, starting with the material that must be eliminated, there is a steady moving forward in the growth of dialogue. First, let us consider further what we shall cut out and why. If your story-playing has been successful, a great mass of conversation has accumulated. Naturally, since the element of time for the production should never be over an hour, that alone would call for elimination. In this dialogue, there will be most uninteresting subject-matter—as well as attractive irrelevant matter. You with your group, should analyze every bit of dialogue in its dual relation to plot (story) and interest. Is this speech of interest to others? Does it tell anything important about the story? Is it necessary for the portrayal of the character being played? If not, it has no place in the final production. It has served its purpose as a release of energy.

In the same way you build with your creative group the dialogue that you do want. You have in mind the beginning, middle, and end of your play. *Each* character in the play must contribute to the art structure of these three parts. Every line must be significant in that it furthers the story and builds action. It must all move towards the climax or story peak and it moves through a series of complications that in turn build crises. This is why I feel that the inexperienced teacher does well to take as her first (and second) creative adventure, a well-known folk or fairy tale. The skeleton is already there for her to build upon. The climax is inherent in the story, together with action and plot. Her task is to build it into a drama—a living creative thing for the children. Whereas, if her choice is from life or social studies, she must first be certain that she has built up out of her facts an actable story with a dramatic line. That is exactly what is the matter with too many so-called plays. They lack all elements of an interesting story; their only virtue lies in the benefits of study creatively approached.

Not only must the dialogue be significant and interesting but it must have life, it must be natural and in keeping with the character. It is astonishing what real, although crude, characterizations children can present with the aid of suggestion and discussion. If they once perceive the fact that we are motivated to every act by either a thought or an emotion, their portrayal of the motivating force that lies behind action becomes real. However, it may not be *our* conception of the character because it is being created by a *child*. Yet if we impose our adult viewpoint it ceases to be a child's play. I cannot reiterate too many times that the teacher is the guide—not the performer. Although the final performance may be more crude than it would be under her detailed direction, it will have life and vitality of its own. And creative growth will carry over to the next experience.

I have said that the words must be fluid. Each day the same fundamental points of the play will come out clothed in new language. It must be borne in mind that we are not memorizing words or gestures—only the skeleton of the story. *At no time should the words become set in a mold.* The minute the dialogue ceases to be fluid, the life has gone out of the enterprise. New points will come out in each new rehearsal, if there is an unceasing fire under the whole creative adventure. Cut and dried drill is never exciting. On the other hand, there is nothing more thrilling than taking raw material and converting it into an artistic product. You have two creative tasks: that of taking raw story material and producing an art form; and that of changing personalities by means of your own creative power. This is not at all the same thing as imposing upon others your own will, artistically or otherwise. "For the vision of one man lends not its wings to another man." One is opening up the mind to those who come to you for inspiration; the other is making tools of those you teach. All creative effort leaves its mark upon those who share in it; and nowhere is the effect upon character more marked than upon children enjoying creative dramatics.

There is another factor in creative direction of plays, the coaching. One is often tempted, when faced with diffident children struggling for expression, to suggest definite actions or words. Except under unusual circumstances do not do so. Let us assume that the class has decided the Queen is angry. Her words must indicate this. Her body and gestures must be in keeping with anger so that the audience has no doubt as to the emotion. If you say: "Stamp your feet and clench your hands," it is only one way of showing anger. But is it the way that particular child in her personification of the Queen would portray anger? We have to keep in mind that not only words and lines must be creative, but that the acting must also—hence the coaching. If you give the matter thought you will immediately recognize the psychological truth back of this. We are all individuals. We all suffer from and rejoice in the same fundamental emotions, yet no two of us express these feelings in the same way. My anger may be cold and smothered; yours explosive; another's may be caustic. Our bodies betray our emotions in different manners. My body may show its emotions in an intensified stillness. Yours may go into action. That is what makes us individual. Personality is unique. No two of us ever react in the same manner to the same stimuli. You may find that this is clarified by thinking of the personality in the following terms: you are a unique organism not only in physical detail, but in every aspect of personality. To accept this fact makes it reasonable that each individual must react to any given situation in his own way. Therefore, think of the child as an organism of the whole. When you insist upon his acting a part as *you* feel, he is no longer functioning according to his own particular make-up. But you have to go a step further and realize that the part to be portrayed may again have different reactions from your own, or the child's interpreting the part. Therefore in coaching, decide upon the emotion and then let it find expression in a natural way. You will get far more variety and far better results because they will be spontaneous and natural.

"How can I get him to act at all?" you ask. In the chapter on behavior problems and rehearsal problems

(Chapters IV and V) you will find specific suggestions for some of your problems.

The fact that children respond so delightfully to the world of imagination does not mean that they are free in the expression of emotion. One of the reasons you and I suffer as adults from stage-fright is that we have not learned to think creatively in new and strange situations. This inability to think creatively may be due to the fact that the situation is new, nevertheless it is fundamentally built upon the "social image" the child, or adult, has of himself. I like the expression because it so clearly expresses the situation. The image the child has in his own mind, of himself, interferes with the clarity of his picture of what he is trying to portray. To make this concrete let me illustrate. Suppose a child, attempting to "get inside of himself" a new character cannot "feel" the part because he is so conscious of the fact that he is before a public that all he can concentrate upon is his fear of what they are thinking about him. This social image may take many forms:

1. A fear of ridicule based upon experience.

2. A desire to please you, as the director. In this case he does not feel free to go ahead and allow the character to take hold of him; he is always wondering if you approve, or disapprove of his acting.

There has been too much of the exhibitionist type of acting in the past. We might list many different social images the child may have of himself. It is extremely important that the leader should know these forms, recognize them, and understand something of how to overcome them. If you understand the power of dramatics as an educational force you will readily see that by the use of creative dramatics the pattern of thinking in a child may be changed so completely that he will have new social attitudes as a result of this dynamic dramatic experience. Acting, in the creative meaning, is nothing more or less than learning to show by our voices, with our bodies, how some one else is feeling in a given situation. If the feelings are permitted to come through the body in a natural way, a manner which is self-expressive to the person acting, it is not difficult to learn to act. We can not, of course, all learn to be actors in the great sense of the word. But we can learn to feel for another by experiencing vicariously his emotions. And an artistic perception will be developed; the play will be life in miniature, so to speak.

Another point to keep in mind is that no individual or group of persons is going to keep the same level of creative sensitivity at every rehearsal. That is to be accepted as part of the game. The teacher should not become discouraged nor permit the group to become so. Rehearsals are the product both of mental activity and emotional response. None of us is at a constant emotional state. We have a rhythm. We feel intensely, then we relax. The same is true of creative activity. The rehearsals will be highly inspirational, then drop to almost, or quite, commonplace level. Do not be deceived by thinking that this means that the resources of the group have reached their end. On the contrary, the time to give the play is at its highest peak. Only then may you and they drink from the cup of joyous success that makes a second creative adventure so much richer than the first.

Chapter III: *Questions*

1. What is the best way to handle a demand for a "Creative" play when time is limited?
2. How are you going to explain "imagination" to your children?
3. How can you tell when your children are truly creative, and when imitating?
4. What is one of the fundamental methods of starting your group to functioning in creative play?
5. Define clearly in your mind the following points:
   a. The essentials needed in your first material.
   b. What is, specifically, *your* function?
   c. What must be the nature of your class questions to stir and keep interest?
   d. How may questions fail?
6. a. What is the function of the story?
   b. How does it relate to the final production?
   c. How can you know whether your story is effective?
7. What is your chief objective in story-playing?
8. Make a possible list of the dangers to the "creative" development in this stage.
9. What do you consider the social advantages of a changing cast? Why?
10. How would you know when your cast is beginning to move out of their *own* personalities into those of the play?
11. Can you enumerate actual happenings that indicate to you when a character is merely "acted" rather than lived?

12. Why may the first imaginative group freedom be confusing?
13. Do you feel certain you have defined the difference between child humor, and adult humor? Why is it essential that you should?
14. How do you know when the dramatic playing is ready for structural form?
15. Why is the dialogue in some plays stupid, in others dramatic? How can you avoid the first?
16. What is the structural form of a play? Where does motivation function? What determines clash? What is *dramatic line* in any play?
17. What are the underlying values socially and educationally of this process of dramatization?
18. What are the constructive psychological results of a good "creative" play? What may be disintegrating?

Chapter III: *Summary*

1. There is a definite relation between:
    (a) Stories
    (b) Story-playing
    (c) Story-drama, the structural art form of creative plays.
2. The real value, social and artistic, in a play lies in:
    (a) The dramatic experience of the individual
    (b) The development of a group by the leader.

3. Creative energy functions not only for the participating group but also for the leader. When a high level of creative work is attained all share in this freeing of energy.

4. There must be a time for creative unfoldment.

5. Imaginative development—and participation—not emphasis upon production as such, is the keynote to successful creative dramatics.

6. Plotless material dramatized is excellent for "limbering up."

7. The director is only the torch who lights the flame.

8. Story-telling is the means by which a child first participates imaginatively.

9. Story-playing is the free dramatization of the story. It is a group process rather than an art form.

10. Story-drama is dramatic experience whereby an art form is created by the group out of action-material.

11. Dialogue and characterization are the outgrowth of motivation, and must pertain to the dramatic line of the play.

12. The director is the leader, but not the dictator.

13. The personality of each child is effected by his total self, and can only function creatively when set free from the social image of himself.

Psychological and Behavior Patterns

In our last chapter we took up the functioning of technique in creative dramatics. Before going into a discussion of the psychological aspects of rehearsal and behavior problems, let us review, for the purpose of emphasis, important points thus far: we have in the past so associated drama with art that the recognition of the more profound meanings of educational dramatics have only begun to receive the attention that they deserve. I have emphasized that we are reaching for a greater depth in our creative work than merely a successful performance. There are, however, certain behavior problems that present themselves in almost every creative effort and they are more readily handled when they are fully understood. It is not enough to have a working knowledge of the procedure in coaching; there must also be an understanding of childhood behavior problems.

Time plays an important part in the creative growth, both of the group and in the individual. This is important from the artistic and the social viewpoint. Always we must remember that the teacher is merely the leader; that she shall not put her own personality to the front as a coach. Rather, she must feel the needs of each child and try to meet them; only thus may she bring about the unfolding of her group.

We have elected to do creative dramatics with our group of children because of the fundamental values in creative play. We have agreed that the underlying need is that of stimulating the imagination. We have accepted the belief that only through group creative effort may this be developed, rather than by means of a dramatic drill that has as its emphasis the final artistic production given for an audience.

How does creative dramatics do this? Within the group are different sorts of cultural background, varied social classes, and every type of personality. When a creative play is undertaken all of this background comes into play. The drama is a slice of life; the actors are the sum of the characters they are portraying, plus their own personalities, unique in themselves, with the problems they carry within themselves. You, as the teacher, are helping these small people, not only to interpret new personalities, but also to integrate the effect of one child upon another. If you, as an educator, have as your ideal the widening of the vision of those under your supervision, all these psychological factors must be taken into consideration. The subconscious is a deep part of life. In what way, if any, is the creative imagination in dramatics directly related to this inner life? Let us again think back upon the technique of our creative drama.

As stated before, "creative" means to build, to bring into being. In imaginative participation in a play, the child becomes an active part of a new environment and to that extent a new person. If properly directed and stimulated, he reaches down into his new personality and brings forth new qualities, characteristics—foreign to his conscious vision—new emotional experiences that are not brought to life or created for the moment only, but become an integral part of his conscious self. He acts not only with his mental and emotional equipment but with his whole body; for every emotion will take a physical expression natural to him. The director, as I said before, does not impose his own ideas of bodily movement; rather the child is creating from within. He is made to *see* and feel the drama of life through his experience in this small slice of life presented to his creative imagination. Because he, as an individual and as a part of the group is creating, this experience becomes to him a psychological unfolding of his personality.

The interplay of personality has a direct effect upon the final play in that as one mind plays upon another, as one imagination stimulates another, different responses are the result, and the plot and dialogue are built out of fluid and flexible material. Each child conceives the imaginative idea of the character he is portraying according to his own mind and in terms of his own personality. He gives out his conception and gets a definite response; through an integrating group the final result is determined.

The story of "Snow White and the Seven Dwarfs" will give a concrete illustration. Suppose in the first scene with the Queen and the hunter Jane is the Queen and Jim the hunter. It may be that Jane has in her mind a very cold and haughty Queen, cruel to the court attendants. In that case, she will present that personality as far as she is capable of so doing.

The creative reaction to that interpretation, on the part of Jim, will be quite different than if he were to respond to a gracious and royal Queen. In addition to the dramatic interpretation there is also the effect each child has upon the other. By that I mean, if Jane is a very spontaneous and dramatic individual she will react differently upon the other child than a repressed person would. That is one of the reasons for changing casts. You cannot in creative work get away from the fact that the play of one personality upon another is of vital importance. Certain individuals set free the creative flow in others; some inhibit it. The final production is the sum not only of individual reaction but of group integration.

A careful analysis of the creative values from the standpoint of social experience will again prove how fundamentally creative this type of drama is in its effect upon the actual life of the child. You, as the teacher, have a golden opportunity to open the gates of life for these children. Drama is a medium by means of which you are going to provide color, form, motion, speech, and even music. You have as your purpose the building of a living and vital life philosophy through the discussion of fine moral and esthetic values. This may be done indirectly by discussion of plays, when all the talking in the world on the same values under different circumstances would only be impatiently received as "preaching." As a social opportunity the play is unusual because every child may participate. If there is no possible way in which Jim may be used in the play itself, there are sundry other and important duties, such as: curtain raising, the making of properties and stage setup, managing costumes, and the business of the last final day. During all the rehearsals the group as a whole must be on its toes to assist in the rehearsals by enthusiasm and cooperation. At the end of the experiment you—as the teacher—should be able to look back and see that you have accomplished the following:

1. Awakened the creative imaginations of the group as a whole.

2. Developed the personality of every individual in your group. This you must look upon as the most important spiritual point of it all. *Creative* dramatics cannot fail to do this if the emphasis is upon the individual, not upon the production as an art in itself.

3. You should also feel an enrichment in your own personality. There is no greater gift in life than the knowledge that one has contributed to the personality development of another. Drawing upon imaginative perceptions, sharpening insight into character and feeling cannot fail to deepen the teacher as well as the pupil.

4. You and your group should be eager to go on to the next adventure. For one of the most fascinating attributes of the creative is that no two undertakings are ever alike. They cannot be because of the constant renewal and growth of the play as the children awaken imaginatively.

In the ideal situation, after choosing a play or story to create into a play, all one would need to do would be—

start! Unfortunately it is not so simple because we are dealing with the human equation. Certain types of children will immediately present difficult adjustment problems. These are:

1. The type of child who has had much instruction and training in an artificial kind of dancing; he is accustomed to the acclaim of the audience and too much attention.

What is the best way to approach this problem from the viewpoint of the leader? Your difficulty will arise from two sources, although the child's mother is the fundamental one. She is enamoured of the idea that her daughter has talent and she has pride in her personal appearance in public performances. She will not recognize the stilted facial expressions and unnatural gestures, the unchildlike attitudes for what they are. (We are now speaking, of course, not of the lovely creative dancing that may so well contribute to other forms of creative work.) When you are ready to cast, this type of child expects nothing less than the lead. My advice to you is to keep the child's participation all a deep, dark secret from the mother until the time of the production. The child will usually cooperate naturally if there is no other interference.

2. The child who has had elocution is equally a problem and for the same reason. Fortunately this type of dramatics has almost gone. However, you may have such a child. Her intonation will be unnatural, stilted, and she will lack all courage to use her native ability, if she possesses any, because she has so long been told what to

do and how to do it. The best way, I believe, to handle this child is, again, to try to get the interest of the child before the production period starts. One of the temptations will be to become impatient with such a child. You must remember that she is not to blame and, therefore, set about finding her creative outlet.

3. Less difficult to manage, but with preconceived ideas, is the child who has had a type of artistic drama where the emphasis was upon the performance. The problem then is that of setting free the child from over-direction.

4. Older children who have had no opportunity for creative expression at all and who are, therefore, inhibited in a physical way must be assisted to become less self-conscious in their activity.

5. A mixed group of boys and girls when ten or over who will take refuge in smartness as an expression of self-consciousness.

Certain personality problems that are directly related to the rehearsals will crop out almost from the first:

1. Inhibition may be due to a general inferiority re-action, to the child's social image of himself. In any case your job as the teacher, or director, is to find out the cause and then build up through creative activity the deficiency in his pattern of thinking. The personality must be unfolded and energy freed by creative forces that give the child happiness.

To accomplish this you must be prepared to help the child to see himself objectively; to obtain distance from himself. This, as has been pointed out, cannot be done by discussing the problem with the child. You need to have the technique and the understanding of the causes back of the difficulty and to work outward by helping him to become the character in the play. Often you, yourself, must obtain what is termed "psychic distance" both to the play and the individual child before you can benefit him. By that I mean you must be able to stand off emotionally from the situation and see it from the standpoint of a director, not as an individual. This is highly important because it will eliminate many discipline problems. You will not be annoyed by personality traits that show up in a rehearsal because you have gone outside the picture and are looking on, rather than framing yourself within the picture. If dramatics is to be the educative force that it should be the leader must be very clear in her own mind just what her relationship is to the group. You must constantly be aware that you are there, not to impose attitudes, but to bring each child to the threshold of his own mind. This cannot be done unless you first understand how to see the picture objectively.

Because a child is inhibited it does not follow that he has no active imagination. He may have a very vivid power of entering into the feeling and lives of others and be quite incapable of expressing it. Such a child needs *help* in order to reach the fulfillment of his powers, for if the emotions cannot find outlet in words, then all his life he will be handicapped by the inability to make others realize his capacity for feeling, and for understanding of their problems. It will shut the child off from living in the most vital sense. Or, a very clever child may attain considerable freedom in verbal expression and be unable to show emotion physically. These are difficult children to start creatively because of their distrust of their own artistic impulses. Every move awaits direction.

To help the inhibited child enter into a world of creative freedom underlying causes must be understood and corrected. It may be a physical handicap in the child. I recall one group which I had over a period of years in high school. On the first day a boy enrolled—a dwarf— and when we began to plan our work my first thought was, of necessity—what shall I do with this child? I could put him into stagecraft or some off-stage activity. However, he wanted to act. We chose "Penrod" with this in view, and he took the part of one of the small colored boys with great joy. The child with the physical handicap must not be kept from acting if he wants to do so. It is possible to take his mind off of himself by means of creative interest so that he loses all consciousness of self.

Or it may be that the child has been the object of ridicule at home, hence is afraid to express himself. Faith in his own talents and conceptions must be built up; it will take a long time to do it but success will be one of your richest rewards.

2. The selfish child desires the center of attention. He must be subordinated to the will of the group as a whole, and should not be given a big part until he has proved that he is ready to work for results rather than for his own glory. These children are difficult to work with creatively because of their lack of cooperation. I found one of the best remedies was to keep presenting the prob-

lems of the *characters in the play*—never by calling attention *to the shortcomings of the personality doing the acting*. We cannot teach anyone to be creative by criticism.

3. The child who is undisciplined in self-control, temper and other personality traits may also be taught valuable lessons. If he sees that the plums go to those who are helpful, he will perceive the value of cooperation. If each time he disturbs the group he feels their displeasure, rather than yours, he will soon realize that tantrums do not avail in drama even if they are successful elsewhere.

4. Bossiness is another unfavorable trait in a creative enterprise. Class discussion of the traits of a bully, with no reference to the child in question, was a successful means of presenting the problem. Or putting him into the part of a bully so that the group could discuss the *character* in the play, evaluating the unpleasantness of bullying, was even more successful. In that way the whole group saw such a person objectively. It is astonishing how quickly the unpleasantness of such a person is recognized when in action. It does no good at all to discuss the person as such.

5. Lack of concentration is usually due to an ineffective imagination. By stressing constantly the imaginative development of the play the quality may be awakened or stimulated.

6. Jealousy is a product of the group where experience has been formal and an audience has played an important part. The creative group plays for joy of the thing. When the problem does arise, attack it by trying to make clear

that the play is a unit—that without perfection in every part it cannot succeed. Each person is subordinated to the whole. I found it wise not to permit the same person to have leads twice in succession. We are teaching a far-reaching lesson by our emphasis on the creative whole. We attain joy through perfection of effort; not by personal triumph over another. I think there has been too much stress in the past upon the lead in the play; upon talent as such. Educational dramatics should not have such an objective.

7. The child with a marked sense of inferiority is going to slow down rehearsals. He is frequently one of the most sensitive in the class. His feeling of inadequacy or his social image of himself prevents him from creative freedom. Give him something within his grasp. See to it that he succeeds to the fullest capacity of his stage of unfoldment. More than that, see to it *that the rest of the group give him complete recognition*. Who may say what the limitations of another person are? If he is given the encouragement of success, that may so awaken him that all his life he will be better fitted for happiness. You are not just creating a play. You are creating the power to live, to be, and to feel. You are offering a richer life through imagination. Drama is only the tool; the means to the end of complete living.

8. The show-off is a relative of the selfish child and the bully. Frequently the former has real originality and initiative that need constructive direction and may then be real assets to the group. Ofter the bully is not clever. All may learn to become a part of the pattern. If the

show-off persists in clowning, disrupting the play, he must be made to feel out of the social pattern by ignoring him. The group will put him in his place because he will prevent them from full enjoyment of the play. That is far more effective than any adult discipline.

Chapter IV: *Questions*

1. What are the essential points of difference between drama as art and educational dramatics?
2. What is the difference between a functioning group and a group of individuals working at the same project?
3. If a child is imitating you, or himself, what are you going to do about it?
4. What do you mean by interplay of personalities and how can you recognize it dramatically? How do you get it?
5. Why—if rehearsals are successful—is there a sense of renewal on your part?
6. How are you going to find out the causes back of the *seeming* failure, in a child or group, of the creative capacities?
7. "Social image" interferes with creative dramatics in how many behavior patterns? How are you going to set him free from this picture of himself?
8. How can you use your group to control behavior patterns during the creative periods of rehearsal?

Chapter IV: *Summary*

1. Each child conceives the imaginative idea of the character he is portraying according to his own mind and in terms of his own personality.

2. Creative drama is an open door to a richer personal life.

3. Teacher problems have their root in:

   (a) Lack of knowledge of technique on your part.

   (b) Artificial training for the child.

   (c) Behavior patterns.

4. Social image is the picture the child carries in his own mind of himself. It is the barrier between himself and true dramatic experience.

Chapter Five

Specific Rehearsal Problems

We have discussed the various types of children who will present many forms of behavior pattern. Now let us take up the ways of meeting these personality factors in creative dramatics.

There are devices that may be used to help overcome inhibition, which is the chief handicap from the point of view of creative activity. There will always be the aggressive, pushing youngster, with or without talent, who is eager to take all the parts. Your concern is not so much with him, but to see that he gets his opportunity without forcing out the more timid and shy child. It may be well, in the very beginning of your story-playing, to allow such a child to play opposite to a timid child. This is often an incentive to the more sensitive or inhibited child, without throwing too much of a creative burden upon him when he is not prepared for success. You must keep in mind that one of the educational values that each child carries away is the feeling of success that is rightfully his. Nevertheless even when the group is enthusiastic, when the time comes for putting into words and action their own ideas, there will be self-consciousness. How can you get a quality of reality into your production in spite of this self-consciousness?

Rehearsal Problems

We have already taken up the discussion of the play as a structure and what our objectives should be to produce an art form. We recognize the value of group action and the importance of proper questioning. However, teachers complain that even so some children are inhibited. Inhibition and imitation are the two great handicaps. They are the result of the mental image the child has of himself. Your task is to find the cause and change the social image pattern. The following are a few common and helpful devices:

1. First, as was suggested before, find out the cause of the child's inhibition. Is it built upon fear? Or is it due to a lack of imagination? Treat it as a behavior problem.

2. Never mention the name of the child who is creating. Call the child by the name of the character being played. This will take the attention of the group off of the personality of the child who is handicapped or is not interpreting his part well and put it where it belongs —upon the character being portrayed. If this is done, the child who is timidly trying to find some expression for his emotions in action will think of himself, not as Jim, but as the hunter or the king.

3. Never say, "Don't do that, do this." Instead, throw back to the class some such question as: "*How* can we express what the Queen is feeling at this time?" Allow the whole group to get up and try to express the feeling as an entity. This is a very satisfactory approach in more than one way. It allows the shy child to be temporarily lost in the class—thus taking away a fear of self-expres-

sion—and it also is very good for the children who want to run the whole play. They have to become a part of the group. During our story-playing period we did a great deal of this. It is astonishing how often the very child, who appeared to have no dramatic feeling, proved when creatively released, to have much more perception than his more aggressive playmate.

4. Suggest *always what the people in the play do and feel*. Never what the real children do. This is fundamental because it contributes to the illusion of the play. You wish to avoid breaking into the imaginative concept of the play. The more clearly the participants dwell in the realms of the play, imaginatively, both in action and mind, the more creative will be the results.

5. When the entire group stand and do nothing, as will sometimes occur, stop and discuss the story again as to interpretation. If one or more characters seem to lose the thread of the story—when you have reached the point where you desire to keep the story as it is and are building for a play—remind them as indirectly as possible of the theme by saying quietly, "And in the story the Queen did . . ." so that the child need not be jerked needlessly out of his creative path. For the sake of specific illustration we will consider the part of the Queen, and look at the small scene where she is before the mirror. She wishes to know who is more beautiful, Snow White or herself. What are the points to be made clear to the audience?

1. That she is the Queen.

2. That she is jealous of Snow White.

3. That the reason for this jealousy is that Snow White is more beautiful than she.

4. That she must get rid of Snow White.

Assume that the child impersonating the Queen says, "I don't know what to do." There she stands, stiff and unresponsive, uncreative. What are you to do to start the flow of creative energy? You are not going to give her specific directions. Your objective is to help her to submerge her own personality in that of the Queen. Let me be more specific. If you think of a personality as a unique organism acting as a whole (not the mind in one direction, and the body another) and there are patterns that would not be expressive of the character to be portrayed, you will have to find out how to make the rearrangement of the patterns. I like the following words offered by Mrs. Chorpenning, of the Children's Theatre at Goodman (Chicago): "Creative acting involves the reconfiguration of tensions unique to the individual." To clarify that meaning let me illustrate. Suppose you have a child (who is by nature very shy but has a fertile imagination) acting the dwarf in *Rumplestilskin*. Assume that she plays the part at first, as she will, with complete repression, even if she has an intellectual grasp of the dominant traits of the dwarf. When you succeed in getting that child to *feel*, on the *inside of her*, and express to any degree some of the real quality of the dwarf, you have begun to make new arrangements within the unique pattern of her own personality. That is why it cannot be said too often that creating a play is more profound than producing an actable structure. It is that. In addition it is the creating of new values in living by participation. That is the fundamental difference in the educational effects of formal dramatics and creative dramatics, and is in line with the accepted educational trends of today. The personality as a whole must be considered, *not the intellectual functioning of the child only*.

How may it be known she is a Queen without words at all? By her walk; by her admiration of herself? By her court? Permit the entire class to get up and walk around in the person of the Queen. That will start pantomime movement, in a group, relax the muscles and relieve tension. Now let one child do it in the Queen's room. If at first her motions are small, as they often are, it does not matter if they definitely express characterization. As she *lives* the part those actions will grow.

"How do we show jealousy? In how many different ways? How does our body act before we say anything that indicates jealousy? What emotion do you want to arouse in the audience towards the Queen? Towards Snow White?" By means of such specific questions, step by step, the character emerges in the mind of the group. The child interpreting this part is relieved of inhibition by becoming the Queen in thought and action. If you continue to have difficulty, there are other ways in which the problem may be solved:

1. By taking the child alone for pantomime work.

2. By changing casts; this has been discussed in Chapter III and more will be said about it later.

3. By doing a great deal of group work until the stiff child becomes lost in the freedom of the group.

4. Praise for every effort that is at all creative. Some children need far more praise than others to build in them the confidence that they are not behaving in a "silly manner." There is nothing more fatal to creative effort than the twin evils of ridicule and sarcasm. Generally speaking, however, the inhibitions that start with the creative project are removed by interest in the play itself.

Timid and Other Difficult Children

Timid children, inhibited children, and those that are shy, all need praise in abundance. They should not be forced, but whenever there is a minor success full credit should be given. On the other hand control your smarty child, who is trying to get the attention upon himself, by calling to his notice and that of the group, when his interpretation of the character is false. Often it is necessary to give him a subordinate part. The idea must be held constantly before the group that it is *the character to be portrayed that is important—not the small part being acted or the actor*. Our play, first, last and always keeps interest alive and creative energy flowing.

Other types who interfere with the creative flow of the group and present rehearsal problems are: the bossy child; the one with no self-control. The former is one of the most difficult problems to deal with in your rehearsals because he wants to tell everyone else just what to do, when to do it, and why. Since that is the very thing you are desirous of avoiding, it is very trying. Frequently such a child does, however, have very good ideas. A constructive channel is the discussion of what the characters in

73

the play are to do and why. As in the case of the bully, it is wise to put such a child into a part where bossiness is shown up in a most unpleasant light. I have said before that we do not point out the fault of the child, but the fault in the character portrayed. Direct criticism in creative work cuts off the flow. In the case of the child who lacks self-control, aim to develop his ability to concentrate. Since he will dispute every direction and throw tantrums when thwarted, he is a very disrupting person to have around. If, however, the flame has been kept burning in your group, they will soon discover and resent his interference. If he persists in his tantrums, removing him from the play is often very effective.

Lack of concentration is often a nervous habit. The child may be helped by giving him very small parts and helping him to succeed in them.

If these remarks seem to be a repetition of some other parts of our discussion, I can only say that from personal experience and that of other teachers it has been my observation that these types are the ones that cause the greatest difficulty in creative dramatics. It is the commonplace problems that get between you and creative expression. It is of no avail to have a knowledge of the result you desire, if you do not know how to bring that end about. And creative dramatics is difficult to handle without a knowledge of technique because of its very informality.

CLASS CRITICISM

Effective use of class criticism is a device that may be

helpful or harmful as it is used. From the first telling of the story to the actual production of the creative drama, it is a group enterprise. For that reason it is inevitable that the children are going to offer criticism. Often the suggestions are extremely good and can be immediately put into use. However, sometimes criticism is well meant, but not wise. Then how can you, as the leader, handle the problem without seeming to rebuff the sincere offering? You may receive it with consideration but defer it to another time; you may put it up for discussion; or you may allow the children to try it out in order to show that it is impractical. The method to use is the one that will best fit your particular group.

If the critic is one who always offers suggestions to feel superior, it is sometimes advisable to allow him to get up and act upon his own ideas. In any creative work one must, of course, recognize that sarcasm will not solve the problem. If every step is carefully planned by the teacher and the group, with thoughtful analysis of all the reason for dialogue, action, and plot well understood, children will soon lose their consciousness of self and be a joy to work with creatively.

Questions From Teachers

1. *How can I keep a large group of twenty or thirty or more children interested for a long period of time when only a small number can be in the play?*

That has been partly answered by the constant reiteration that the group must be a social unit. Every member of the class shares in all discussions. Also that choice of material enters into the success of this enterprise. The technique must be followed so that there is a real creative growth at each and every rehearsal. When the action fails to develop along new lines, but becomes an imitation of that already learned, it is an indication that there is not enough discussion. The group is too easily satisfied, and so are you! There should be no imitation of what has been learned. When the children begin to repeat the same lines and act out the same gestures the creative life has ceased to function. New questions must be thrown out constantly; new points of characterization must be developed; and life and vitality must be constant.

However, there are ways that will make the going easier. It is often a wise plan to do all one's stage-craft and costume work before starting upon the last and final step of what is to be the perfected production. The age of the children will dictate to some extent the procedure in this matter. Stage and costume should be an integral part of the creative performance. Starting half the class upon this work while the other half acts, is effective when possible.

There is no way to keep a large group of children quiet and orderly over a long period of time in dramatics, any more than in any other subject that takes individual attention, unless they feel that every part of the play is dependent upon them. But if casts have been varied, and all other rules adhered to, and you enjoy it all, no big problem will arise.

2. *What shall I do when I am suddenly told to have a creative play ready in three weeks?*

Your happiest answer to that is to keep the informal type of story-playing going throughout the year. In that case you will always have ready some material that may be finished and delightful without stress and strain at the last minute. If you do not have something on hand, you cannot, in three weeks give a creative play although you may offer a creative program.

3. *What can I do to lighten the nightmare quality of the dress rehearsals and last performance?*

Plan from the very beginning in your own mind for this event. Unquestionably there is nothing more exhausting than a dress rehearsal and final performance for which one is unprepared. I suggested in an earlier chapter that one of your means of keeping the children occupied might well be in starting the stage properties before or simultaneously with the creative drama. This has the obvious advantage in a large group that has not had the benefit of creative dramatics by providing occupation for the whole group; it offers a constructive interest, not only for the cast but the class as a whole. If it is possible at all, have all the duties attendant upon a play assigned to the more muscle-minded children, such as:

Raising and lowering the curtain.

Stage-property committee, whose duties are not only to have gathered up the needed things but have them in the right places at the correct time; even quite young children can do very well at this.

Costumes to be got out and put away may be another duty of a group. Arrangement of the stage itself and the making of many things to be used. All of this can be distributed among various members of the class to the advantage both of the students and the teacher.

Dress Rehearsal

It is desirable, if possible, to have three dress rehearsals. The first is a walk-on rehearsal in the place where the final play is to be given. By that I mean that all major properties and settings should be used to make the surroundings familiar. The second dress rehearsal should include all properties and, if possible, all costumes. Little children find it very amusing to see one another in a costume and there may be a certain amount of buffoonery the first time. Also those who are to assist in the technical end of the stage plans now have a chance to function in the same tempo as the final affair. You are working now towards the climax of happiness that has so long been anticipated by all and plenty of time should be allowed so that the children will not be under any pressure. Each child should know his exact duties. When the third and last rehearsal comes, if possible do not have it the day before the play, but allow one day to come between.

The reason for this is that nothing you can do in the way of corrective measures will now be effective, and that one day of rest often gives renewed vigor. This last rehearsal should go off as if it were the play itself. Do not interrupt the creative flow. If there are mistakes, jot them down and speak of them later. Remember that the children will have to meet emergencies the day of the play, so permit them to do so now. Leave the performance on a high note of pleasure and anticipation. I do not subscribe to the saying that a poor dress rehearsal means a good performance. On the contrary, what has not been learned by the time of the dress rehearsal it is now too late to learn.

FINAL PERFORMANCE

Arrange for plenty of time to get the children ready to go on as there is nothing more fatal to the creative flow than to feel uneasy at the last minute. I have found this procedure to be helpful with young children: arrange enough chairs in a row for each participant to have one. Upon these chairs hang the costumes in the order of use (if more than one is to be used). Have the child fold his own clothes as he removes them and place them upon a newspaper beneath the chair. If the child is old enough to read, his name should be pinned onto the chair. If not, a picture to identify him. This careful plan will do away with a great deal of the confusion that is so trying and unnecessary.

If the committees have already been assigned for the stage and property care, have large wooden boxes at hand. Place in these boxes the properties, when possible, in the order of their appearance, and have only one person responsible for them. In this way there will not be any lost or misplaced things at the moment when they are needed.

As has been stated, each child has already practiced his duties at the dress rehearsal. If he can read, the directions should be written down and pinned on the walls of the dressing room. The boxes must have a definite place and be marked as to the scene in which they are to be used. The scene shifters should have exact instructions as to which direction and where they are to remove their properties so that the oncoming things may be brought on from the opposite side; this avoids confusion and speeds up the time element. Long waits in plays are not necessary, and the audience is justified in resenting them.

If there is to be make-up, a table in the center of the room should have all the necessary items laid out upon it. A small semi-circle of chairs drawn up around this table will do away with the running around that is too often found in a rehearsal and which is very destructive to creative mood. If the children are very young, have someone tell them stories until all is ready. A last and very important suggestion before you are ready to undertake the final performance that is now to take place in a few minutes is this: *do not give last minute instructions.* The children now know the story, it is fresh in their minds, and anything that is said at this point will only serve to close the creative doors. Send them into the performance with the spontaneous hope that all their joy and yours of the past few weeks will serve to intensify and light the creative flow of the story. Sit back and make-believe a bit yourself. Watch those who now come into a wider plan of life; enjoy those who are animated by an unfolding of themselves; see the creative flow go through the children. Now you can reap the sowing of your seeds of development; the harvest is in the enrichment of personality that has come out of this social and artistic enterprise.

Chapter IV: *Questions*

1. Of what devices can you think to overcome:
   (a) Inhibition (created by social image)?
   (b) Timidity?
   (c) Lack of concentration?
   (d) Bullying?

2. By what means can you use effective and constructive class criticism?

3. What is the essential problem presented in a large class room? Can you devise means of overcoming these problems?

4. How are you going to plan a successful dress rehearsal? What are the usual failures?

Chapter V: *Summary*

1. Careful analysis of the behavior patterns within your group is essential to successful creative directing.

2. You, yourself, must obtain *psychic distance* from the group and yourself. This means the ability to see the individuals and group dramatically functioning. By the latter, to view them without personal emotional reactions. Only in this way can you see the manner in which the group can become a creative unit functioning artistically.

3. Destructive and constructive class criticism and how to use them.

4. Teacher devices.

5. Suggestions for dress rehearsal technique.

Chapter Six

Creative Directing

We have discussed the original play, its material, the approach in technique and the psychological values. Now let us consider, briefly, the coaching of a play already built. Keep in mind that no young children will derive from this play the same social values that come from the creative play. However, among older boys and girls, it is the usual form of dramatics. Therefore although this is a manual primarily for building the technique of the creative play, I do not feel that it will be complete without a discussion of the creative methods underlying all educational dramatics.

Not all directors of educational dramatics use the same method. Nevertheless, today there is more and more emphasis placed upon the natural approach of the individual to the interpretation of the play. We shall find that many of the same principles apply to the directing of both types of dramatics. The essential difference lies in the fact that in the purely creative play one has only the outline, which must be filled in by means of characterization, motivation, meaningful action that builds towards a climax; whereas in the formal play, the art form is already complete and it is the job of the teacher to help both the individual and the group to bring to life the play—with the cast as the interpreters of the characters within the play.

One of the faults of the average amateur school play is that it is not a living, vital thing. It is often a polished enough rendering of lines, but it lacks reality. In order to draw out from the actors the best that lies within them, there must be a keen awakening of the imagination on the part of the actors. The play must be viewed as a slice of life. It must present itself to the audience vividly. Therefore creative coaching is to build toward the goal of naturalness. Again the group must as truly create together as in the creative story-play. The director shall be what the name implies: one who by means of skillful questions draws out the meaning of the play, in the manner most natural to the individual interpretating the part. You—as the teacher—may give a polished final performance if you use your own art sense from beginning to end; if you direct each gesture, each move upon the stage; if you offer your interpretation for each action. However, you will not have produced a creative play, nor will your group be advanced one whit in ability to take the initiative in the next play. Moreover, unless you are a skilled director, your play will have many stilted moments in its production.

How then shall you go about rehearsals? Before you select a play be clear in your own mind as to whether there is any value in the play from the viewpoint of: emotion, art, and pleasure in production. After you have selected your play read it aloud to yourself. Do so until you feel yourself taking on the emotions and movements of the characters. This may seem to be a great deal of work, but if action is the result of the whole self, how can you "get the feel of the actors" by an intellectual approach only? You need to actually feel in your own muscles a reaction to the part; and keep in mind that you are to feel what the character is to feel, *not* as you would feel. You get your first lesson in this matter of psychic distance. One of the reasons for the shallowness of much of our amateur acting is due to the belief that inexperienced actors must have a "light" play. Also the fact that interpretation is too much an intellectual appreciation of the play without realization that emotion must be actually felt to become real, even during a play.

Second, read the play aloud to the group. Permit a free discussion from the standpoint of interest to the future audience, as well as complete understanding by those who will take part in the production. At no time should a play descend to the dullness of drill. It must be fired with enthusiasm from beginning to end or it will not be the joy to you and to the participants that it otherwise should be. A knowledge of the fundamentals of play production, on the part of a teacher, will greatly help in achieving such a goal.

COACHING PROCEDURE

Discuss with your students the types of people within the play, what they are doing and why. *But do not decide at all upon any action to be taken.* This must be worked out by the actors themselves as the play unfolds upon the stage during rehearsals. *All emotional reactions and physi-*

cal expression of those emotions must be coordinated.
It is the failure to do so in an inexperienced group that
so often gives to the amateur play a lack of vitality. Life
is not a separation of our faculties into the physical,
mental, and emotional. We think, and in thinking our
bodies express through movement, or lack of it, what we
are thinking. There is always the outward evidence of
the inner disturbance; we are angry—we express it according to our own nature. We do not work out ahead of
time the exact portrayal of an emotion. We may, it is
true, be working for an effect. But even so we have in
mind the *emotion* that we desire to arouse in our audience, not the manner of exact mannerisms by which that
emotion is to be expressed.

After an open discussion, whenever possible allow
freedom in casting for the first time or so. I have found
over many years of teaching dramatics in school, settlement and playground that a flexibility of casting was
very beneficial from several viewpoints. It enables the
teacher to observe her group in action, it permits the class
to see more than one person interpret a part.

At this point should be discussed the try-out. There
are occasions when a try-out is necessary. Yet in some ten
years I did not use that system. Is it not true that if we
have the highest ideal for educational dramatics in mind
that we are thinking in terms of the development of the
individual and the group as a social unit? In that case
we need only to look closely at the possibilities in try-
outs to see some of their defects. One is that the most
aggressive and outstanding children are, by the very

85

nature of things, going to grab all the parts. The sensitive, but often gifted child stands aside; or, if he participates, is too inhibited to make the most of the opportunity—hence he fails to obtain the part he might very easily grow to. Hence my early experience taught me that one of the most serious mistakes a teacher may make in the creative realm is in just this manner. Ofter a very glib and seemingly talented child quite failed to develop into the creative person I had expected him to be. This may have been due to overconfidence, a shallow nature, or because he has had "leads" too often. On the other hand some of the most gifted actors have been boys and girls almost too shy to speak at the first trials. They have found themselves in the field of dramatic art. To play a small part sensitively will give them a feeling of success that is more valuable in their future adjustments than any other one factor.

When a class was new to me, I found it best to allow time for becoming a little free before making a final selection of parts. If we were planning a series of plays to take place over the year, even if some of them were only to be class plays, by the time we were ready for a real production every member of the class had been given the opportunity to be in a small part. In this way all had shared in the social experience, and the class itself was now capable of choosing for the big production those best suited to the parts. We made these decisions on several counts: talent, ability to work, reliability in the matter of memorization, attendance at rehearsals and willingness to do whatever was assigned. We had an invariable rule that the same person could not twice in succession hold the lead in a play. The reason for this was that if dramatics is to be *the means to a social development*, all must share in the creative enterprise. At first this created dissension because, unfortunately, too often the talented child has year after year led the production. In the end, however, the class itself felt it was the fairest way. Also by this method each individual rotated activities; all were on the stage-craft or the costume committee during the year. Thus each received a well-rounded insight into the routine of a little theatre.

COACHING STEPS

After the cast is selected rehearsal starts. The first two or three should be uninterrupted as advised in the discussion of the creative story-play. The actors must get the feel of the play, the characters and their emotions. Just as none of us hopes to know another person in one or two brief glimpses, the characters in the play cannot be revealed all in a minute either. There may not seem to be any character development at all the first time or two except in smoothness of line reading. This is all right. If a bit of characterization is caught, that is fine; but do not suggest to the pupils. Let their understanding grow. It comes through "dramatic experience."

One of the first steps in creative coaching is to have in mind the *values* of the play, and your part—as the teacher—is getting them out. It does not follow that because you are not imposing ideas that you do not have a clear and definite understanding of the values within the play. You must know the high points in each act and scene—who the important characters are, the mood and tempo of the whole, and the inter-relation of each. Each part must be delicately balanced in your own mind. What is the theme? Without a mutually clear idea of the dramatic line of a play, it is impossible to play it correctly since the interpretation of the entire play depends upon emphasis. Therefore you, the director, must be certain what that inner meaning is and have it before the group from the first play reading. What is the climax? What are the moods of every actor in the play? What emotions are to be portrayed? How can you get stage balance without dictating movements? What is the author's intention in the play? I mention this point because sometimes comedy is played as farce, and the two are not the same at all. One is humor—the other exaggerated humor. In comedy there are two types: broad comedy that is played much more broadly, and thoughtful comedy. The later produces laughter but only because of the human element stressed. Many a comedy with character parts has been ruined because the director failed to formulate the true values of the play in her own mind.

FIRST STEPS

There are two vital points to be understood in the first two or three readings of the cast: one, the actor must begin to feel the character he is to live and be during the weeks of play rehearsal.

Second, the large movements of the group must be established. By that is meant: large crosses, grouping for the sake of dramatic emphasis and beauty of line. The first must come by actual dramatic experience upon the stage, through muscle reaction and emotional feeling. The later will be arranged by you largely. All crosses, movements and so on must have a definite reason. That reason may be to give emphasis, to isolate the center of interest, to give beauty of stage, to make meaning clear. Each move must be logical, either for stage meanings, or because of emotional feeling. It is the natural outgrowth of the emotional state of the characters. The actor should understand just why the character he is interpreting makes the move or gesture that he does. We see immediately that if every move is the result of motivated action, these large moves will be natural, hence both spontaneous and remembered. *No move should be without a logical reason.*

After these large movements that effect the grouping upon the stage and bring together certain actors for emotional reasons, the next step is to bring about the refined or small gestures and moves of each member of the cast. Here again pause and remind yourself that in order to create a character time is essential. Assume for the sake of clearness that you—as director—conceive a character to be a certain type. If you mentally impose your concept of that character upon the child, he will not be creating. Only by giving him the freedom to create from within will he truly become—for the time that he is within the play—that person. Better that he renders a cruder presentation and that it be his, than that he put on the mask of your conception of that character. Each act of the character must be taken under consideration. For exactly as in life, we are affected by the emotions and thoughts of those around us, so also is each person portraying a part affected by those who play opposite to him.

All through the period of play rehearsal, which we suppose will be at least six weeks, there should be the constant use of discussion. Thus is reached an understanding of the characters, their feelings, minds and being. Every gesture, every inflection of voice should be an outgrowth of that new personality until the character is so definitely living that the whole play assumes life. Only thus can the untrained actor achieve that which is vital and living in his performance. He must *be* the character. If sympathy is to be expressed for the Queen, then permit the feeling to be portrayed as the child feels—not as some one else does. There is, however, one thing to consider. Be sure that there is a definite and clear understanding of the author's idea of the character; being creative in coaching does not mean license in interpretation of the play—and this interpretation must not be fuzzy in the minds of the actors.

There are a few outstanding faults usually to be found in the amateur play. The cues frequently drag. This slows down the whole play and often detracts from an otherwise excellent performance. One may, however, use certain devices to obtain quick cues. From the very start it should be clear that the only time there is a pause between spoken lines is when there is dramatic significance to a pause. Then the pause must be filled with action. If not, the lines must come with precision—just as in real conversation you do not have long and awkward pauses without reason. To insure speed, try the following: clap your hands before the one who is slow has an opportunity to get in his line; thus he is trained to get it in ahead of your clap. Bear in mind that this method does not mean hurrying the line itself—only the cue.

2. Try to say the line before he does.

3. Make him repeat correctly until the timing is accurate.

4. Develop a tempo sense.

Another outstanding flaw in many productions of young players is the lack of variety in tempo. This may be attained creatively by emphasis upon the *mood* of the play as a whole and the mood of the individual character. To be specific: a sad play moves with a slower tempo, yet it must have variation to bring out the climax. Intensity of scene may be brought about either by slowing the tempo or by speeding it up. The question may well be asked, why is that a matter of creative coaching at all? Is it not just a matter for the director to decide? The answer is that a real feeling on the part of the cast will bring about a real understanding of tempo. Tempo is a matter of mood; mood is an expression of the feeling of the part. If a child has built up within himself a sensitive perception of the values within the character he naturally feels a swift tide at one time, and an ebb at others.

Another pitfall in coaching is the control of inhibited movements and imitative type of acting. To overcome the former, again I suggest stressing the creative aspects of building the character from within rather than imposing a form from without upon the one acting. In other words let the character do the work—not the actor. Other times it may be necessary to coach the inhibited person alone to change the pattern of his social image. Get him to enlarge the tentative movements by using some such suggestion as: "That is a good gesture (it may be small but a true portrayal of the needed emotion as far as it goes) but it will not be seen from the rear of the room." In such a manner also you may be creatively preparing your group for the audience. Your questions may well include some such suggestions: "Are you making the feeling of this character clear to the audience? Will those who are watching catch the significance of the move you just made? If not, how can you enlarge it? How many ways can you think of to portray the emotion that you have in mind? Which best pictures the character?"

In regard to imitation, what are you—the teacher—to do when one of your participants asks (and he will) "What am I to do now?" Before answering that question let me explain that there are two types of imitation. Namely, of oneself, and of a suggested acting procedure. The latter cannot happen if the entire growth of the play has been through discussion and has been a slow growing creative effort. Nor is an actor apt to imitate himself in that case either. However, at times it does occur. Sometimes as a result of insecurity or social image—so that the child seizes upon any praise of the teacher and continues to do the same thing; or it is based upon an actual over-direction on the part of the teacher. You have failed to get "psychic distance" to the problem and are putting in too much of *your* own personality. Just as it takes more patience to create a real story-play than to dictate one, so also it takes more courage on the part of the teacher to let a play develop than it does to have it all worked out in her own mind and just see that the ideas are carried out. You—the teacher—should have a clear and definite idea of what you desire to accomplish in the play. But you must bring it about by means of indirect suggestion or inspiration; not by dictation.

To coach creatively is a larger job than merely to produce a play. You must enlarge the whole imaginative conception of your group. Encourage discussion not only of the character of the play, but seek a better interpretation of character in the life around you. Then you will find that when you are ready to produce a second play your group will have been enriched not only artistically but in life values. When the actors are allowed to illuminate their own experiences in the light of the play, they see with greater clearness the things that are significant. The group again is functioning. And whenever you have a group creative enterprise that is an integrated experience, you have not only the sum of your artistic ideas, but those of all the participants. Therein lie the educational implications in creative dramatics.

Another problem is that of memorizing. Again the fault usually lies in hurrying the matter. Both the group and the teacher have the tendency to feel that the play will not be ready unless the memorizing is done early in the production. This is not the case. Under no circumstances should amateurs learn their lines before they have developed their stage business and felt the character as it is to be. In fact the more thoroughly the character is "lived," the easier will be the memorizing. The reasons for this are sound because: the minute one separates lines —thoughts—from action, an unnatural situation has occurred. Each movement in life is associated with thought and emotion. We do not decide to walk; we move with the thought. We do not decide to feel; we feel and show it. Each bit of stage business depends upon the motivation of thought; the thought is in the dialogue. Therefore, if the actor has his script with him while he works out all the fine details, he will be unconsciously memorizing his words in connection with his gestures and emotions. Then when he gives up his script he will already have learned most of his lines. Polishing may then be done, deepening, enlarging and intensifying with the knowledge that it is one whole—and there will be no forgetting. Memorizing by rote, and memorizing by living the character are very different; in the case of amateurs it often, if not always, determines the difference between a vital play and a dull performance.

This is one of the most vital points to carry out in successful creative coaching; it is the open sesame to good memorizing and to spontaneity. Drill, alone, will never accomplish the same results. If the objection is made that "I can't act and carry something in my hand" there is a trick in that too. In the child's script, all parts should be typed on paper one-half the size of regular business paper. These scripts should contain only cues and the lines of the person acting—no other. Like this:

Cue (line containing last thought as well as words) Here I am.

Line of character—Huntsman, I will tell you something . . . etc.

Cue—I will give you a reward.

Line—But Snow White is such a beautiful girl.

All cues should be underlined with red. Do not put directions upon the acting sheets except for exits and entrances. Only your copy contains everything and space for notes.

When the actor carries this small script, which is bound with large clips, he can keep his thumb on his cue line. As soon as he hears it and speaks his own line, his thumb moves on to the next cue. In this way there is no waiting while the student hunts for his line; he memorizes his cue along with his lines, this is essential for a good performance. Often he can get along for pages without it, yet he has the psychological assurance of having the script with him.

It may be well in this chapter to say something about the prompter. Whenever the age level permits, much may be accomplished by using one of the class as a prompter. It is a very responsible position, and one that the person assuming should have from the first rehearsal. In that way he grows with the play, understands all the tempo changes, knows when the actor makes a pause and when he is struggling for lines.

It is possible that your first play will not be as polished as you desire, but your second will show growth and with each new one, style will develop and creative power. One other problem occurs to me as needing attention in coaching. Be sure that the exits and entrances are sustained in the character parts. By that I mean the illusion of reality is furthered in a play when the characters come on and go off in character.

If you have the courage to stay with the creative approach, you will, before long, find that your group is easily able to surpass others in the lifelike quality of its performance and in addition is genuinely dramatic. We must never forget that an appreciation of drama, rather than one successful performance, is the goal. Educational dramatics, whether in the form of story-playing or in creative coaching is a joy to the teacher—and to the children.

Chapter VI: *Questions*

1. What do you consider the greatest psychological fault in most creative teaching?

2. Do you believe that a play should be chosen with a profound meaning, somewhat beyond your group, or do you think an easier play is a better choice?

3. What is the part of the audience all through rehearsals?

4. What value is there to you, the director, in reading *aloud* the play to be coached, before presenting it to your acting group?

5. Why is a high degree of creatively growing power a result of group discussion? Does that mean the same thing to you as intellectually analyzing a "part"?

6. Just what do you mean by "dramatic experience"? How do you know when you are obtaining it?

7. How are you going to create variety of tempo?

8. How do you obtain "psychic distance"?

9. What are the educational implications of creative directing?

Chapter VI: *Summary*

1. The play must be directed creatively to produce a living, vital performance.

2. The characters can only be real and living when they have become part of the actor. This may be accomplished through discussion, and actual dramatic experience.

3. Directing may be divided into three parts:

    (a) Exploratory stage.

    (b) Fixing.

    (c) Aesthetic.

4. Amateur plays may be highly artistic as well as educational.

5. Devices of technique are necessary to the director to produce results.

6. Memorization is a matter of psychological rather than intellectual approach.

Chapter Seven

Suitable Dramatic Material

We have already taken up the matter of using daily dramatic incidents for practice; also we have indicated what material is most advantageously used in the story drama. Pantomime, as one form, is excellent as a source of creative material. In elementary form it is a mere group exercise in portraying rudimentary traits of character; or it may be used as a means of freeing the self-conscious, through group participation; on the other hand, it may be a complicated presentation of material in a series of pictures in action. For pantomime is, of course, action without words.

Let us look at pantomime from the standpoint of a group exercise. We shall use as our illustration a group of children going on a picnic at a lake. Since these are young children, we shall simplify the material to their needs. How are we to start out so that pantomime will have significance as an exercise? The objective is to differentiate the people within the group. How are they shown to be different? By individualizing them. Therefore allow each child to assume one outstanding character trait such as: happy, grouchy, funny, angry, and so on throughout the range of emotion. Having decided upon these traits, how are they to be portrayed, without words, so that the rest of the class may recognize them?

Decide what is done upon a picnic—how would each character react to the given situation? How can his body show it—through movement, hands, posture, all the mannerisms that go to make up a person. Pantomime is an excellent means of learning detail of characterization because action, not words, must make the meaning clear to the audience.

Pantomime is a very definite aid in overcoming the inhibitions both of the individual and the group. Because the group acts as a unit (as in a mob scene), hence the inhibition (lack of freedom in words or body) is removed. Frequently also pantomime subjects are pure fun. Pantomime, when used to portray a complete story drama had best be let alone until great skill has been developed by your group as well as creative alertness on your part. But simple pantomime is most useful as a means of attaining spontaneity of bodily freedom.

PAGEANTRY

A pageant is a story told in dramatic sequence and given as a spectacle. It is as definitely a dramatic form. It may be simple or very elaborate. It does not in any sense fill the same educational need that the original story-play does. The material for a pageant may be drawn from several sources:

1. Historical: this type of material may represent:
   (a) Various phases of some one period of national or local history. One might take for original

study some aspect of the life of Lincoln, the Gold Rush, or immigrant life.

(b) It may present in chronological sequence pictures of the entire history of a place or a people. Such as Indian history, Spanish California, or any other dramatic legend.

(c) It might choose as its story episodes from the life of a national or local hero; such as Lindbergh and his early flights, Columbus, Madame Curie, etc.

2. Industry and its development lends itself very well to a dramatic and social evaluation of material; and may be very colorful if taken historically. Life in the old Guilds, or in various industries.

3. The use of Biblical material offers many opportunities for varied pageants; such as variations in the interpretations of Christmas customs throughout different lands, scenes from some parts of the Bible and the many possible symbolical interpretations of its teachings. Stories built around Bible meanings as illustrated by "Why the Chimes Rang" lend themselves to lovely pageants. I have used the latter in great simplicity with a group of twelve, and again with two hundred in the cast.

4. The pageant may be based upon a literary subject; mythology or fairy tales. "Sleeping Beauty" makes a beautiful pageant.

5. For very small children you can work out a delightful Mother Goose pageant; and the dramatization of a folk-tale combined with music and dancing makes for a very attractive effect.

6. The seasonal pageant, although overworked, especially along the conventional lines of the return of the seasons, may, nevertheless, be lovely when used symbolically. Festivals, anniversaries, and folk pageants are not only colorful but free from artificiality because of the simplicity of theme.

There are definite values in pageantry, especially for the older groups. It offers the opportunity for a large group project, with creative possibilities for many. However, the danger in so spectacular an event is that the creative aspects may be lost sight of in the effects sought; the whole becomes a matter of strain and drill; the individual a sacrifice to the perfection of detail. A pageant, by its very nature, is always larger and more elaborate; with many costumes, stage properties, and preparations. These activities may be the source of successful assets in the social project but too often degenerate into a striving for perfection, against time, with unhappy results for all concerned. There is no reason why, with proper organization, even an elaborate pageant should not offer great joy to all. Every creative effort, no matter what may be its nature, should leave the participants, and the teacher, with a sense of inner renewal; of having found within himself unsuspected resources upon which to draw. I cannot reiterate too often that it is only when the leader ceases to create that the job becomes a burden. The leader must bear in mind that to depend upon only her own inner ability is to limit herself; rather must she draw upon the composite flow of the energy released by the whole creating group.

Another vital point of consideration in the pageant is the audience. The audience, for an original or creative play, is there largely for enjoyment. In the pageant audience that is also true, but at the same time the audience is there to see a spectacular affair, not primarily an educational one.

There are several types of presentation possible in the giving of a pageant. But the age of the children, the purpose of the affair, the place and the number in the cast all determine the manner of giving.

1. One of the simplest ways is to have a dramatic reader who, as the story is acted in pantomime, reads the story. The reading of the story must be spaced to meet the action.

2. The entire performance may be in pantomime, using large placards, with captions, to make clear the story. This is very good for little children in something like a Mother Goose story.

3. You may combine the use of speaking parts with tableaux effects; or with moving action. "Why the Chimes Rang" illustrates this type. The play may take place on one side of the stage; when the climax comes for the little boy to see the church, all the rest of the stage may be a beautiful and moving pageant with only music accompanying.

4. The entire pageant may be composed of speaking parts.

5. Pantomime, music, dance and lines may be combined. In general, the younger the children participating the less speaking there should be.

The technique of production in a pageant is quite different from that used in creative story telling. It is, as I have already said, more elaborate in its use of numbers, color and accessories. It is meant to be a spectacle of beauty and movement. It may be a closely woven set of stories or it may be loosely bound together.

There are also certain differences in the coaching of a pageant. Often in a large pageant the entire school or playground will be participating. In this case the work is probably divided among a group of leaders. However, there may well be times when one teacher will be called upon to produce the whole. Suppose you are to give "Sleeping Beauty." The cast is to be divided into units for the sake of ease of management:

1. The speakers
2. The pantomime group
3. The dance group
4. The singing group
5. The stage and property group
6. The costume group

Since you cannot possibly have all of them going at once, yet must, in this case, meet a time schedule, the best procedure is to divide into groups for the first six (if possible) rehearsals. Do not attempt to have all units there each time of rehearsal. Next combine two groups, adding units as fast as possible. There need not, if this method is followed, be more than three full rehearsals. These three must have lights, properties, and stage as they are to be in the final production. The last two rehearsals should be complete in every detail. If this were always

103

planned for and carried out, much of the strain of last rehearsals wuold be removed. When all the groups are to be together have a definite place for each group, with a leader assigned for each. All properties, and so on should, as said before, be in place. If the children are very little, have mothers to help you.

TABLEAUX

Tableaux are pictures without words or action. Pantomime has action but not words. Pageants are pictures with, or without words, in action. Tableaux when effectively used, may be very lovely. The use of color in costume, lighting, and massing of the figures to make a dramatic picture is an impressive form of drama. It takes much less time than other forms of drama and has very little to do with developing personality, but the tableaux is often useful to portray something desirable in a significant manner. In order to avoid the set and lifeless effect tableaux so often have, do the following: after your details of the picture are worked out, and each child knows not only his place in the picture but also what he is to portray in feeling, instead of holding the positions from the moment of setting the picture, give a signal just before the curtain rises and allow the group to move into position at that signal. There will be a more lifelike effect if this method is followed.

GESTURE, MAKE-UP, AND VOICE PROBLEMS

Make-up for little children should be as simple as possible. Of course, where the performance is large—as in a pageant and hence in a big place—there must be some make-up. When it is used it should be done so as to preserve the natural effect. Rouge, lip rouge, and eyebrow pencil will take care of all but the character parts. In the smaller creative play all we aim to do is to keep the illusion of reality. Characterization should be made effective through costuming and action, rather than depending upon heavy makeup; however, you must be guided by the situation.

In the matter of voice work we have several difficulties to face: There is the very timid or feeble voice that will not carry. The too loud and unmusical voice—trying to the ear. It seems unwise to work on the voice as such, because it makes the child self-conscious. The voice may be worked on indirectly by several different means. The whole group may work on some simple exercises that they will look upon in the light of play. The fundamentals of a good speaking voice are breath control and relaxation. If these two principles are adhered to, there can be very little seriously wrong in the voice placement. Any tightening of the throat muscles, tongue, palate, chin, back of the neck, along with a failure to take long, deep and sustained breath will result in a wrong placement. The words should be said sharply but not with effort, against the teeth.

Yet since you are not going to discuss the matter with the children, how can you attain results without doing so? You can say: "Let's all sit up straight. Take a giant breath. Now let it out in an easy yawn. Now let's count in a whisper." The whisper should be heard by you from the rear of the room. Then hum—with throat easy. Chant such words as sing—bing—ring—. Say such syllables as le-li-lo-lu—lightly and easily. Then work for the *feeling* the voice should have by your interpretation of the character.

Consider first the child who speaks too softly. Why does he do so? Largely because he is timid. Calling attention to that fact will not correct it. But if you sit in the back of the room and smile at him, then say that you cannot hear what *the character* is saying and that you want to enjoy the play, he will speak up!

Take him alone, if necessary, but at no time refer to his voice, only to the fact that the character is not heard. If, on the other hand, the child has a loud and unpleasant voice, again determine whether the cause is physical or psychological. If the latter, refer to the nature of the character portrayed and call attention to the fact that by too loud a voice he misinterprets the character. If a child is completely immersed in his part, his voice will take on a sympathetic timbre with very little guidance.

As to gesture—action must be the logical outgrowth of feeling. I believe, however, that you can never say enough against the gesture that is a *made gesture*. It is, and will always be an unnatural one. Each of us, however small, is himself. To tell the child to make such and such a gesture is to handicap him at the start. Begin with the emotion. There are, to be sure, a few technical points that even young children can understand about the stage: They can know front stage, back stage, wings, the meaning and significance of exits and entrances; they can be taught not to stand in front of one another because it spoils the view of the audience. They can understand grouping for the same reason. This is a much more logical and natural reason for action to little children than a technical one.

Very little children cannot, of course, be subtle in their acting. Mood, tempo and characterization come to them, as does the voice work, by means of understanding their parts. The more thought is given to the naturalness of the whole creative adventure, the easier will be the rehearsals and performance.

Chapter VII: *Questions*

1. Why has pantomime a definite social value?
2. Do you know the difference creatively between a play and a pageant?
3. When would it be wise to use tableaux rather than a creative play?
4. How can you help the child with speech and voice difficulties through the creative approach?

Chapter VII: *Summary*

1. Pantomime is a good medium for obtaining group freedom in dramatics.

2. Pageantry is a spectacular rather than educational form of dramatics.

3. Tableaux are entertainment rather than dramatics. However, they have an aesthetic value.

4. Voice work for small children should not be technical. Instead the voice should be worked upon indirectly by emphasis upon the emotional content of the part.

Analysis of Stories

Dialogue cannot be given in this suggested list since it is already agreed that dialogue remains fluid and changing in the play. However, the suggested play may be studied in more or less detail by means of outline. This will give to us some idea of what essential points must be covered and what left out. You will find an illustration in the detailed account of the procedure in the play "Snow White and the Seven Dwarfs" (*See* Chapter Nine).

JACK AND THE BEAN STALK

If this is to be only story-play the children will be given complete freedom in bringing into play all the different aspects of the story. The story will follow along about as it goes in the reading material. Start at Jack's home—we shall see the peddler come down the long lane —which may well be the aisle of the school room. He and Jack may go outside to look at the cow before making the purchase. The mother goes to market (or Jack, as is decided) for the sake of making the sale. When Jack goes to the house of the giant he may make as many trips as the story designates, carrying off each magic gift, as in the story. All of this worked out freely will provide a vast amount of dialogue and action from which to build the future play.

Now what must take place when the play is ready to be taken up? First of all, the audience must be considered. Not from the viewpoint of the perfection of the play but from the standpoint of interest. What will be of interest to those about to see and hear the play? The stage will be considered, its limitations, and the time element of production. The range of time might be from twenty minutes to one hour. The age of the children, their attention span, and story interest will not permit more than this.

After the length of time has been decided upon, the points to be covered in the play must be chosen. What is suitable to the stage? What points are necessary to the dramatic development of the play? Obviously all the scenes enacted in the story-play cannot be given in the drama. There is not the space, the need, or value in all of them. *Hence an outline of the dramatic high spots should be worked out—each crisis leading to the other (suspense) and pointing towards the climax.*

Divide the play into three parts for the sake of clarity. Part one, or act one, will take place within Jack's home. What are the essential points to be covered?

1. Setting—how are you to make real to the children the setting?

By a discussion of the period of the play. What would peasant people have in their homes? What kind of a stove? Where would it be in the room and why? In what way does such a room differ from ours? Most of these points you have already discussed in the story-playing period. But there is now the problem of elimination.

The setting is controlled by the usable space and by its significance as a means of interpretation to the acting group and the audience. What does the cupboard mean in the play action? Where is the window and why? The audience must be able to see the peddler and Jack look at the cow, out that window. In the story acting it was legitimate for the two to go out doors and see the cow, but in the play itself this is not feasible. Yet it is important that the audience imaginatively "see" the cow; hear all that the beggar and Jack have to say about its sale, since that is an important part of the motivation and plot. *The whole point of the first act is for Jack to get the magic beans.* I shall take this up further in the analysis of dialogue content. (Chapter Nine.)

2. Points of action to be covered: there are certain things that must be seen by the audience to make the play clear. We think of these as scenes.

(1) That Jack and his mother are extremely poor; so poor that their one source of gain is selling the cow in order to have food in the house. The setting will give part of this, but dialogue will give more and it must do so in an interesting way. It is not sufficient for the bald statement to be made that they are poor. The audience must *see* and *hear*. They must *feel* with Jack and his mother. How can this feeling be built up in the audience and in the actors? By the selection of *interesting detail*, this is always the way to eliminate extraneous material that may have grown up in the story-play. The dialogue must not consist of a reiteration of the fact that there is no food in the house, but must progress from that fact,

to the question as to *how* this condition may be remedied. *Scene 1:* Perhaps the play opens with the mother preparing breakfast. Considerable pantomime may be given before there are any words at all. What may she be doing? Seeking in the cupboard for food—set the table—show her own grief. Then in the scene between the mother and Jack the subject of the lack of food may arise. For the present the matter of characterization may be eliminated, although in the end that will determine how each character will act in the given situation. Jack may show his dissatisfaction with what there is for breakfast—then take up the problem of how to handle this; also the selling of the cow. Next, the conversation may concern who is to take the cow to town. And why? *There is a dramatic reason for the right way in this case.* The mother must take the cow so that Jack can receive the beggar. All this is to be *motivated* in the dialogue.

In the story-play, more than likely the group desired Jack to go with the cow as the story does, and meet the peddler upon the way. However, when this becomes a play there is a good reason why this method is not practical. The stage limits us. The whole of the first act must take place in the cottage for the sake of simplicity. Moreover, there is nothing intrinsically interesting about taking the cow. The interest is in:

(1) The returns from the cow.

(2) The way in which the peddler gets the best of Jack.

(3) The beans.

Hence we build up our conversation around vital

111

points in the play so that now the mother leaves. In this way the teacher throws open class discussion by questions. That is her means of keeping alive intense interest in the creative growth of the drama. Every bit of dialogue given *must* have a dramatic reason back of it. It must forward the play, keep the climax in mind and in itself be exciting.

When the play has come to the place where Jack has decided, or had it decided for him, that he is to stay at home while his mother goes, we are ready for the peddler. *Scene 2:* Naturally there can be only a very brief period of pantomime by Jack alone on the stage before the peddler's arrival. There is nothing significant that Jack can do to fill in time.

What are the points to be covered in the conversation between Jack and the peddler? What *purpose* does the peddler serve dramatically? He is the means by which the magic beans are to come into Jack's possession. And Jack either takes them because he is stupid, or because he feels that he is doing something for his mother. That is a point to be decided by the group while defining the traits of the characters. The conversation between the peddler and Jack will embody certain essentials; namely, shrewdness on the part of the peddler and slyness. How can this be shown? By what means does he find out about the need of the household, and how is the audience made aware of his plans to take advantage of Jack? In what way is the cow shown, (remember the window) and what are the points brought out about the beans? How is Jack finally made to take them? When all this has been accomplished, we are ready to return to the mother.

Scene 3: The dialogue between the mother and Jack will revolve around the mother's happiness in the fact that she has found a purchaser for the cow; the revelation that Jack must make that the cow is gone; and what he has in exchange. The mother gives her reaction—despair and punishment for Jack. His remorse. He may fall asleep and awaken to find the beans that his mother threw out the window—have become the beanstalk ladder.

Characterization must be decided as far as fundamentals of character are concerned at the outset. There are several possible interpretations of the character of the mother and Jack; upon those traits chosen will rest the way in which the two will build up their dialogue. Certain points in the drama must be made clear, the play *creates* itself by the *reaction of one personality upon another*. For instance, if the mother is a whiney, spineless person her reaction towards her situation will be quite different from that of a strong person. Each of these mother types would in turn create a different Jack. Or she may be a loving and kind mother. In every case she will have a definite effect upon the reaction and character of Jack. Jack may be a lazy, good-for-nothing as some stories portray him, or he may try to be a good son. He may try to be a good son, and still be stupid. Upon the combination will be built up your dialogue. Also the *way* in which things happen will, to some extent, be determined by the characters.

A popular interpretation of many groups seems to have. Jack an easy-going but rather lazy, good natured person. The mother is rather severe in type. The children

seemed to feel, after much discussion, that such characterization made the story truer to the facts; that is, Jack took
the beans because he was gullible, but with the intent to
help; while the mother went to town because she feared
Jack's lack of bargaining judgment. Later in the story
the action of Jack in taking the giant's things seemed
more logical because of these innate qualities.

Important things to remember are: that every point
in the story must be logical; that all dialogue must *further
action* and *build* towards the climax; and that all this be
done creatively.

Act two in the play will of necessity be in the house
of the giant. Again we find there will be a difference
between story-play and drama. In the story-play the action
will be more detailed. Jack may wander over the hill tops
looking for the castle that he sees in the distance. He may
converse with the man who tells him what the castle is
and, finally, come to the house of the giant. In the story-
drama, due to the natural limitations of the stage, we
must find him immediately at the house of the giant.
What are the points to be covered here?

1. How can he get in? By making friends with the
giant's wife?

2. How can the audience know of his wanderings?
By his disclosures in conversation to the wife of the giant.

3. What can the conversation be about between Jack
and the giant's wife, since there is nothing interesting in
the mere fact that she is feeding him? It may concern
the return of the giant—his hatred of human beings—the

danger to Jack—hints as to the riches the giant has in his possession.

4. The return of the giant and his conversation with his wife. The element of suspense may reach a high peak here by having Jack hidden in a large box while the giant mentions smelling human blood. Jack can keep peeking out. Herein lies both audience suspense and humor.

5. In order to avoid a tiresome repetition of material this act will of necessity be condensed. The story, as we recall, has Jack return home three different times, bearing treasure. That is all very well in the story-play, but it is easy to see that in the drama it would prolong the time of the play and add too much uninteresting detail.

Condensation of material may be accomplished by having the giant sleep following his meal with the magic gifts by his side. Since he will not use all of them at the same time, he may sleep between times or even go out. While he is asleep, or out of the room, Jack will come out of his hiding place, grab the gifts and conceal them. Because the harp will call out "master," it must be the last to be taken and is the *cue* for Jack to escape down the ladder. Each time that Jack steals the magic gift, his hiding of it is made highly dramatic and, also, he is almost discovered at it. In order to bring this about the giant may awaken, partly or wholly, at the critical moment when Jack is in the act of stealing. Suspense is built up this way. At the final escape, just as Jack is ready to go, the harp will call out, the giant's wife enter, the giant awaken. The curtain will go down on Act Two with

Jack disappearing, the giant in pursuit, down the bean stalk.

Act 3: This act will open with Jack as he comes down the bean stalk outside the window. He will be calling his mother to come to his rescue with an axe with which to cut down the ladder, also to take the riches. Therefore the following points in action and dialogue must be made clear:

1. Jack's lines must make it clear that the giant is following Jack.

2. By actions and lines the audience understands that the giant is to be prevented from reaching the end of the ladder.

3. The riches will be explained and rejoiced over.

4. The play will end on a note of satisfaction for the audience in that all goes well for Jack and his mother ever after. (*Note:* it is possible to have a rope ladder covered with paper leaves—this may be a class project— or a real ladder, if the other is not feasible.)

RUMPLESTILSKIN

This story is particularly charming for a slightly older group of children as it has great possibilities for character-ization. Not only that, but it is highly dramatic and lends itself to every aspect of costuming and setting. In the early stages of story-acting great freedom may be attained by the children. The miller, his wife, and daughter, all are excellent material for acting. The court scenes are delightful and when time for elimination of material, much can be retained, always remembering that what is retained is for the build up of interest.

Let us assume that:

1. We have a limited space on the stage. Much must happen in view of the audience. Therefore the most exciting events will be selected for presentation.

Scene 1: The courtroom—with courtiers assembled for the purpose of hearing that the King is about to choose a bride. This scene may be greatly enhanced by having the courtiers assembled first. The purpose is two-fold, namely, to add to the atmosphere by a dance and to serve as the informers to the audience of the King's intention to marry. Suspense is added by having a discussion of the planned-for marriage before the arrival of the King. It is in the nature of gossip. What sort of a person is the King to choose? Will she be from among themselves? If so, which? and so on. At the entrance of the king all will bow before him; there is a flutter among those present to see who will be chosen.

Scene 2: The miller and his wife now arrive. Not content with bearing a gift of flour from their mill, which they claim is the best flour, they brag that their daughter can turn straw into gold.

The reason that I said either the wife or husband may be the braggart is that in one experiment the child *playing* the part of the wife was the aggressor. It was so much more humorous with the miller as the hen-pecked husband that the action was developed around the bragging wife. The original story has the miller the braggart but there is no dramatic reason why the wife cannot assume

117

the role; the possibilities for clever action are increased in that way.

Scene 3: We must have, not only the king's reaction to the miracles the girl can work but also that of the courtiers. What is going to be their feeling? How may it be shown? What is the emotion of the daughter over all this?

Scene 4: The girl is put to the test. If she succeeds she is to be queen; if she fails she dies. To make the stage effect easier and avoid having too many changes of scene, have the courtiers and king leave the stage—and the straw brought on. This is very effective. If the girl succeeds in turning the straw to gold she is to become queen; if she fails she dies.

Scene 5: The dwarf appears when she weeps at her inability to change the straw into gold. Suspense is worked up by the method of his approach; it may be secretive until he is upon her. There is an opportunity here to do some really delightful work with the character of the dwarf. It should be highly creative. The character is developed imaginatively; dancing, expressive of the mischievous type he is; facile expressions portraying his gnome-like quality; a voice that gives the same elfin feeling should all be worked out. It takes a gifted child. The first time the dwarf asks for the gift of a ring. When he receives it, he turns the straw to gold—then leaves. There is opportunity here for more dancing. (*Note:* The straw may be easily turned to gold by having an electric cord run along the floor and the light hidden under the straw; the light to be turned on at the proper signal. If there is amber paper under or over and around the globe it will produce the effect of gold.)

Scene 6: The king, attended by his court, comes to see the miracle. His greed is aroused; he asks for another basket of straw. This intensifies the suspense of the play. The dialogue will be built around the excitement of the court and the marveling of the court.

Scene 7: The girl is in greater despair. Half-heartedly she tries to imitate the actions of the dwarf as he changed the straw into gold. The fact that she fails builds up the sense of excitement in the audience. There is a chance here for some excellent pantomime. A little dance suggestive of the one that the dwarf did, some incantation, all lends imaginative power to the play. When she fails, we find the mischievous dwarf at hand. All the way through, the audience must feel that he is working towards a goal and not that he is freely giving. This time there will be a definite hint in his dialogue that he is going to get her into his power; and on her side the feeling that the future will take care of itself. This time he gets the necklace.

Scene 8: The king again enters. His increased delight is expressed in a greater greed. Once more he orders a basket of straw—to the despair of the girl.

Scene 9: This time, when left alone, she makes no effort to change it herself, but gives herself over to despair. The dwarf will be gleeful with his anticipated victory. His teasing will be malicious. She has nothing now to give him. It is at this point that he asks for the baby that will be hers after the marriage. Here is an excellent opportunity for highly creative acting. The contrast between her fear of failure, as balanced against her unwillingness to promise her baby; the cunning of the dwarf; her desperation that finally results in promising.

Scene 10: In the last scene the king finds the gold; calls the courtiers. The pages announce that the king has chosen the miller's daughter and a dance closes the scene.

ACT TWO—*Scene 1:* The king's palace a year later. The queen sits beside the cradle singing a lullaby. The object, for the sake of contrast, is to present a scene of security. The king enters, asks about the child, and also to state that the king and queen of the North will be here in three days for the christening. The dialogue sets the scene for the future action. The conversation should be of content. In one play by a group of children a delightful touch was given by the entrance of the miller's wife with all of her bragging about her clothes, the baby, the fact that she is mother of the Queen.

Scene 2: The dwarf enters unseen and pops up beside the baby, frightening the queen with his laughing threat to take the infant. The dialogue is built around the following points:

(1) The promise.

(2) Her attempt to offer other things and his refusal to accept anything else.

(3) Finally, his promise that she may have three days in which to find out his name. If she succeeds she keeps the baby; if not, he carries it off. It must be made very clear to the audience that the dwarf doesn't expect her to find out, and that he is merely prolonging the time

of anticipation. She, on the other hand, will be driven not only by the need to save the baby, but that of keeping the king from knowing of the promise. This scene has great possibilities for drama and suspense.

Scene 3: The queen sends forth her pages to find queer names.

Scene 4: Each time they return with a list she is sure that one of them is correct.

Scene 5: In contrast each time the dwarf comes he is more certain of his success. His glee and her despair are excellent dramatic foils.

Scene 6: This will be a separate stage scene but, because of its simplicity, may be played in front of screens set before the queen's room, or as a separate scene. The setting is the woods. Dim and eerie lights are about. The two pages are listening to the strange little man whom they have just seen. He is bending over a little fire in a pot. Then he dances with glee—comes back and chants. This scene may be as comprehensive as the combined imaginations of the teacher and elf can evolve. Of course during the chant he tells his name.

Scene 7: Back in the queen's room. The pages arrive. Breathless. They tell the Queen of the scene in the woods. All the action and dialogue are now filled with her hopes and the contrast that the king makes by coming to inquire how the christening is progressing.

Scene 8: The dwarf comes, gloating. The climax of the scene goes up and up, and yet must not be hurried, until finally the Queen says his name. His rage sends him screaming from the room.

ACT THREE—*Scene 1:* Back in the throne room. The King and Queen courtiers, and all await the King and Queen of the North for the christening. The final gorgeous scene of christening.

SLEEPING BEAUTY

Sleeping Beauty lends itself not only to a drama but to pageantry. There are several ways in which it can most beautifully be presented.

As a play it would divide into three acts, with two scenes in act two. Act one takes place in the court room of the King's palace where the christening is to take place. The settings are:

(1) The throne.

(2) Table and small chairs for the fairies, and the cradle. There must be a screen of some sort for one fairy to hide behind.

The cast is composed of the King, Queen, prince, the old woman, and the princess. The seven fairies complete the group. The scene must include: the reasons for summoning the fairies, the explanation of the royal setting of the table. After the fairies arrive, the giving of gifts, during which the ceremony is interrupted by the old fairy who was forgotten and who now curses the child. The dialogue is built up by the consternation of the parents and other fairies. There is ample room here for both action, speech and pantomime. Sending forth the heralds with the proclamation that all spinning wheels are to be destroyed.

ACT TWO—*Scene 1:* Seventeen years later in the attic of the old woman who has not heard of the King's proclamation against the spinning.

    1. The princess finds the old woman.

    2. She asks the old woman what she is doing.

    3. She attempts to use the spindle and hurts herself according to the prophecy and falls in a swoon.

    4. The coming of the King and Queen, and attendants.

Scene 2: Back in the court room.

    1. The princess is laid upon the couch.

    2. The good fairy makes her sleep happily.

    3. All leave her and are to be put to sleep for a hundred years. It is not necessary for this to be shown. The dialogue will take care of it. This scene should be short and lovely. The fairies may close it with a dance about her couch.

ACT THREE: The royal couch may be outside if desired and surrounded with a hedge through which the prince is to come. Her one attendant is beside her. The prince awakens her with a kiss. The court attendants, in their quaint costumes come awake, and the play closes with a court dance.

In dividing up an act we have scenes whether a change in setting takes place or not. Each *happening* is a unit, or scene. It comprises:

    1. The introduction of a new person, emotion or climax.

    2. Any act is composed of numerous scenes.

Creative Dramatics for Children

Chapter VIII: *Questions*

1. Do you see clearly that there is a definite change between the story-play and drama, due to the needs of the audience?

2. Is it clear that in any story when the structural form is to be considered you must first decide upon the following:
   (a) What comprises the Beginning (Introduction)?
      (1) Scenes in the beginning.
   (b) The middle (body).
      (2) Scenes.
   (c) End (Resolution of problem or dramatic line).
      (3) Scenes.

3. Do you realize that all dialogue has the following purpose?
   (a) Delineation of character.
   (b) Clarification of material for the audience.

4. That motivation actuates every act of each character?

5. That "clash or conflict" may be:
   (a) Physical,
   (b) Mental,
   (c) Emotional,
   and that it leads to the climax of the scene, act, and finally play?

6. That all action by the characters is the outgrowth of:
   (a) Motivation plus their unique personal reactions as a whole.

7. Do you see that the group must discuss these together and *act them* if the play is creative because no one character determines the play?

8. That no play can exist without a *dramatic line* or problem, around which all else centers? This "line" may be:
   (a) The growth or disintegration of a character.

    (b) A theme.

    (c) Pure story-action.

9. How are you going to "plant" future happenings?

10. Of what value are lines that foreshadow further clash?

11. What relation do you find between gesture and characterization?

12. How do you know when you are obtaining true creative results?

13. Are you clear in your own mind that the acting of the play grows *out* of the lines? And that the technique of play-writing must be kept constantly in mind as the two are interrelated. The lines of the creative play are a result of the union of technique, and group acting.

14. If your play is uninteresting is it because:

    (a) Of the material chosen?

    (b) Faulty directing?

    (c) Lack of writing technique?

15. Wherein does the Social-Study dramatization fail as a play?

16. What comprises a scene?

Chapter VIII: *Summary*

1. Find your "dramatic line" or significant meaning around which the play is built.

2. Dialogue then must further the meaning of the play.

3. Sequence, or scenes must be considered constantly in relation to the climax and to each other.

4. Contrast must be obtained.

5. Delineation of character comes through dialogue by means of a careful analysis of motivation and dominant traits.

6. The audience is a participating factor.

125

Chapter Nine

Research in Creative Dramatics

This chapter is a presentation of material drawn up for research. It included remarks upon the material and an exact copy of the progress of the two groups under observation. In presenting this study of two groups of children from varied environments in their attempts to produce the same play (built upon the story of "Snow White"), actual fact material is used. The relation of rehearsal, final outline, and production, will illustrate similarities and differences in the two groups; one drawn from a well-to-do church, the other from Hull House. Structure, climax, plot, characterization are compared in the two and the final production taken down verbatim. All material, for the sake of clarity, will be referred to as A (church group) and B (Hull House) groups.

The method of procedure was the same in each group. The story was told to the children as a complete fairy story. No attempt was made to suggest any acting or structural form. The next few rehearsals were devoted to story-playing. Certain general characteristics were common to both groups. Both wanted to act every detail in the story but had little or no sense of the relationship of one event to the other. Material incongruous to the adult mind did not disturb them. For example, group A had a very complete and modern imitation of a movie wedding in the same rehearsal in which they had the dwarfs take Snow White out into the deep woods "to get some fresh air, while they could protect her." Broad, low comedy was very marked in both A and B, and it is of interest to note that in both groups many of the same happenings served as the basis for humor. The scene with the dwarfs at the table (before the discovery of Snow White) seemed to amuse both groups. They made great sport out of eating—seeing who could spit the far-therest—both groups did this. Extreme harshness on the part of the queen proved a source of amusement. A third common point for horseplay was the death of Snow White at the entrance of the prince. Also the scene between the queen and her handmaiden, especially that in group A, bore the stamp of modern times. The hand-maiden felt no reluctance in demanding more wages from the queen, if the latter displeased her.

From the first rehearsals, through the story-playing period that is essentially a developing period, the two groups reacted to certain definite principles. Each group was affected by the interplay of personality, personal experience, and other material. Also, the incongruous material was a result of two things: a sense of humor, and a drawing from other sources. This humor, unlike the trained adult humor, found expression in horseplay and changed very little throughout the entire period of development. A child who is truly creating will be so lost in his new identity that his acting self will unconsciously select material dramatically fit (natural functioning of the dramatic instinct in all of us).

To illustrate: compare the two Snow Whites. The child in group A was keen of mind, but not so imaginative as timid and shy little Snow White of group B. Group B, as a result, had a much more tender attitude towards their Snow White. Again the play of personality was interesting in the development of the relationship between the two queens and their respective handmaidens. In group A, the haughty little queen demanded allegiance from both her lady-in-waiting and her huntsman. In group B there was a charming comradeship between the two and this is clearly seen in the lines of the plays.

Imagination is shown by children taking two parts. It is of interest to note how one child taking two parts will be different in her characterization and responses not because she is directed to act "differently," but because she feels the two characters as separate entities.

The effect of personal experience had, if anything, an even more direct effect upon the play. In both groups the bringing in of modern material was very pronounced. This was shown by the queen in group A. The smoking and movie suggestions came from the cultured (?) group, and the livelier imaginative work came from the settlement nursery children. One of the most attractive illustrations was the delightful formal Italian wedding directed by the little queen from group B, also the decision of the dwarfs to get a fortune teller to ascertain all about Snow White. Another touch was the peddler who was indeed a street-crier from off famous Halsted Street. Hence it is seen that both personal experience and per-

128

sonality interplay directly affect the creative interpretation of the original play.

A third important factor was the unconscious selection from other fairy lore and its dramatic application to the immediate need. Both groups carried over "The Three Bears." Also both groups interpreted the finding of Snow White and the poisoned apple by the prince much as in "Sleeping Beauty." One group drew upon "Why the Chimes Rang." The job of the leader is to coordinate the spontaneous material offered by the children, train them to see what and how things relate to one another, and to understand plot and structure.

In assisting these children from the free-play stage into the more formal, the plan followed was that outlined in this manual. To assist in obtaining characterization for the dwarfs, definite traits were assigned: the quarrelsome dwarf, a greedy dwarf, the curious, the kindly and so on. (This was before the Walt Disney picture). Then the child was led to see how the character-portrayal of his part must definitely contribute to the structure of the play. The queen's haughtiness and crossness should not be just an experience of fun, but must lead directly to the cause of Snow White's banishment. And that vanity was behind her wickedness must be shown as a motivating force. It was noted that the children in group B, from the first, had a deeper sense of values in the interpretation of character and a keener intuitive sense of structure. Whether it was because this group was less devitalized creatively by the movies, I do not know. There had been less artificial stimulation certainly.

129

In both groups a sense of climax and suspense was found in individuals, but on the whole these had to be developed. To illustrate—the dwarfs, upon their return to the cave, would immediately rush to find Snow White. The beginnings of a natural feeling for suspense in group A came at the third rehearsal, while they were sitting at the table tasting food (Three Bears), when one child suddenly saw finger prints. There was some delightful originality in both groups, illustrating the different trend of imagination in the reception of Snow White. The dwarfs in group B passed the queen's house and saw the queen asking her mirror who was most beautiful. A direct structural feeling towards suspense and climax was shown here. The dwarfs in group A had heard the story "down town" or in the newspaper.

Both groups, A and B, followed an outline in the rehearsals and in the final results it will be easily seen in what ways they differed. The rehearsal material traced the development and processes of a group of widely differentiated children in reaching towards creative expression. (*See* Appendix) As has been stated, they were directly affected by the interplay of personality, personal experience, other material, and merely led by the director. The whole was an authentic expression of what children feel and think dramatically, hence very different from a superimposed and already-created play.

It will easily be seen that of the two plays group B's (*See* Appendix) was superior in structure, imagination, and interest. The two have points of likeness in dialogue and characterization, yet group B remained more consistently in the illusion of the play. Yet both were crude first efforts.

The audience played an important and vital part in the play. There was a responsiveness between listener and actor. Both created. Group B presented their play before a child audience. Their minds and emotions were, there, in key with those of the acting children. On the other hand, group A had many adults in its audience. The result was that the children were made aware of themselves by adult laughter at parts of the play that, to the children, were not funny. The illusion was broken. If the reader will compare the two plays it will be seen that the rehearsal material is richer than the performance. This group A had more to overcome in the first place in spite of a better background. They lacked imagination, were disorganized, and all their dramatics had been of the formal type.

The audience affected both groups enough so that much rehearsed material was left out and new brought in. Compare the dialogue of the dwarfs in the opening scene. In A, the dwarfs left out entirely the sign of the finger-prints. Suspense was lacking, whereas in B, we had a more varied conversation among the dwarfs leading to the climax. In group A the children left out all description of Snow White. Group B, on the contrary, kept to the center of interest in the story because they were imaginatively alive. Group A were not creating in this scene; they were merely repeating what they remembered from rehearsals.

The next scene was more creative. The child taking

the part of the queen in group A became more creative as the play proceeded. She forgot the audience.

Some of the material in the group B presentation was created during the play. The center of interest was adhered to, but the dialogue was spontaneous. The conversation about the bodice was entirely so (page 174) and was not considered funny by the children. Since the audience was composed of children, no break in the illusion came. In group A the adults laughed at the remark, "People look to be kind, Snow White, but they are not." The result of the laughter was to make the actors self-conscious and bring on sterility of imagination.

Scene four of group B contained a fascinating illustration of how the dramatic sense, while creating, will adapt itself to a new situation (page 176). Due to the fact that some of the parts were doubled, it was impossible to have the Queen change her costume as had previously been planned. The Queen was obliged to appear in her disguise. The Queen and her lady-in-waiting, without any coaching, improvised their dialogue so as to make it carry forward the play action, adapting their imaginations to the demands of the new dramatic situation. The group A Queen in scene 7 (page 158) also quickly converted her dialogue into an explanation of the huntsman's absence when he failed to come. A delightful little original dramatic touch tieing the play together is Snow White's longing for the huntsman and Letitia, the maid, and the use to which the Queen put the knowledge. In this same passage it was interesting as to why the child connected the red apple with California. (page 177).

Another effect of audience reaction was in the closing scene of group B (page 178). The children were weeping over the form of Snow White when one of them happened to look around. He suddenly became conscious of the audience. The prince had a velvet cap with a plume; it was the first time he had worn it. The prince snatched the hat off his head, threw it on the floor with a grand gesture. The audience rocked with glee; the weeping dwarfs were entranced. The prince snatched the peaked cap of a dwarf, put it on; the dwarf wore the plumed hat rakishly. Then came realization and the lines "He shall not laugh! Our beautiful maiden is dead." This brought the play back into its forward movement.

The reference to gold (page 179) is from "The Queerest Name in the World." The children had seen this play a few days before with a similar scene.

Another interesting point of comparison is that of the A group, who were not content to close the play without seeing the queen avenged, while B group were contented with the marriage of Snow White.

The value of these two plays, which were very crude, was the spiritual and mental benefit the children derived. The happiness, particularly of group B, was worth all the time spent. This happiness was a deep-seated one coming from self-expression, from release in their present environment to a higher imaginative level. There was not a child in the cast who was not a richer personality as a result of the concerted creative effort. Some children who could hardly be induced to speak at first later took part. And these children were not unique; all groups worked with since then have had more or less the same inspiration. Teachers who use this method are enthusiastic in their reports of results.

If one of the reasons for creative dramatics is freeing the child for a richer life, through imagination, these plays most certainly succeeded. The real value in such an effort lies in carrying the group through a series of plays wherein the development can be traced and a finished product result. This experiment was carried out a number of years ago when creative dramatics was indeed in an experimental stage. In fact the purpose of the research was to make a study of just such original work.

Chapter Ten

Creative Teaching

If he is indeed wise he does not bid you enter the house of his wisdom, but rather leads you to the threshold of your own mind.

In this quotation from *The Prophet* lies the meaning of creative living, out of which may grow creative teaching. It is not sufficient for you, the leader, to know your material. The underlying significance of creative teaching is much more profound and complex. Your value as a teacher, or leader, in the world of education may be said to depend upon your ability to bring each child to the threshold of his own unique capacities. Beyond that you cannot go. But if you understand the philosophy behind all creative living and teaching, you may be a great teacher. Not always in the sense of being an authority in your own field, but in the wider field of living a life fully.

For in these words you accept the fact that each individual is unique unto himself. That he is the sum of all his past—racial and environmental. He is an organism that in its entirety functions as no other human being in life can function. There is no way to change the elements that go into the making of a unique personality. But there are ways to rearrange the pattern to better advantage. But it can only be done by the creative method. No other person can *impose* upon another a deep inner change. That must come from within. In exactly the same way you, the teacher, cannot change the unique personalities of the individuals whom you have the privilege of leading, by imposing knowledge. But you may by creative teaching open up the gates so that each person may approach *in his own way*, the threshold of his *own* mind. Only thus can you hope to further genuine thinking, balanced emotional living, and an enrichment of the whole personality.

How far from our usual approach to teaching this concept of the uniqueness of personality is! You may be a great teacher or you may be a mediocre one, not because of what you know or do not know intellectually about your subject, but by your presentation of your material— your own creative approach. The teacher is far more than one who disseminates facts. Creative teaching is an art in itself, whether applied to the teaching of dramatics or of history—or merely teaching children the fundamentals of a family relationship.

To lead you to the threshold of your own mind. Interesting experiments among the feeble-minded have shown that even a poor mind, when creatively functioning, can learn something. To illustrate I will relate briefly the results obtained in a large institution for the feeble-minded. The children had never been permitted play, in the sense in which normal children play. It was considered impossible, because they were so destructive. After a period of experiment, play was introduced, even

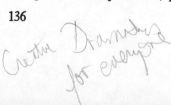

among those of very low intelligence. It was done from the creative standpoint. A pageant was created in which children of such low mentality took part that in the Maypole dance they had to have the children tied together and literally guided around the ring. But the point, from the standpoint of creative living, and teaching (for the two cannot be separated) is that those children, who had never before done *anything*, succeeded in giving a group performance created from within. Low as the intelligence quotient was, it was functioning.

If personalities with so low an intelligence can create, how much more may a fine mind be opened to the varied facets of learning if it is taught to use, not the wisdom of the teacher, but its own potentialities.

> We teach and teach
> Until, like drumming pedagogue, we lose
> The thought that WHAT we teach has higher ends
> Than being taught and learned.
>
> *Augusta Webster*

Opposite to the feeble-minded is the very bright child we all have seen, whose brilliant mind is closed to all creative effort because the mind has been taught not to think (create) but to accept unchallenged all material presented to it. Such a child will accept and reach out for only such material as is fed to it by the teacher. Such a child will not have a conception of using his own unique endowment for the greater end of relating knowledge to life. Yet with creative teaching, all children may, to some extent, learn to do this. To open

137

wide the minds of the children is the function of the teacher. The results obtained are the rich reward.

What is the purpose of creative teaching as applied to dramatics? In earlier chapters this has been discussed, but again let me reiterate that the primary purpose is to open the minds of your students so that they may, for themselves, enter into the world of imagination—may discover that which is unique that lies within. And mind is not just the intellectual capacity to learn facts. It is the ability to make the most of the entire self—emotional, spiritual, physical, and intellectual. Without this integration the personality will fail to be effective. If you have this goal in mind for your teaching, it will be the foundation of sound thinking. But since this book is concerned fundamentally with drama it may be well for us to consider the function of creative dramatics.

You may ask yourself, what is the difference between creative teaching and what you might term "scholastic" teaching. Could you say that the latter is concerned with the teaching of facts? And that it finds its greatest reward in the response of the parrot-like pupils who may have keen intellects? Such a student may be brilliant, he may have the capacity for originality, yet he may have no conception whatever of the working out of his own personal type of thinking. Such a student is the one who often is a brilliant scholar but who later does not fulfill the promise of his student days—because he has not learned to analyze, examine, and synthesize what he learns in relation to life. If, however, he learns to function as a whole, creatively, he is able to accept life and see himself as a part of it.

The teacher who is working creatively sees the fine mind of a potential scholar and is not satisfied with filling that mind with facts. She will see to it that such a mind is awakened to the value of the knowledge itself. Such a teacher will not be happy until even the more limited minds among her students have been aware of the joy of creative activity. Just as the feeble-minded children were led step by step to a degree of normal activity, so must you lead your students to the gate of the awakened mind.

Your specific functions as a creative teacher are:

(1) To estimate the student's potentialities.

(2) To have the vision yourself to plan a concrete project whereby each student may be led to develop his own abilities to the utmost.

(3) To be an inspiration to the student, not by your dynamic personality, but by inspiring him to belief in his own power and the ultimate success of his own creative effort. This may need great wisdom and understanding on your own part. For you must be able to have that quality of what I termed "psychic distance" both for yourself and for him.

Let us consider, in detail, the first of these functions. In every class there will be a wide variation in the types and depths of minds represented. Not only will there be intellectual variation, but also differences in individual emotional capacity, and in experience. This is your raw material for your dramatic work. It presents to you an

139

unusual opportunity to learn of the child's abilities and capacities. By the process of group development you have an opportunity to help the individual child change his patterns by creative living under a new environment (play) in a new character (part). He is aided in overcoming behavior patterns, such as self-consciousness, by changing the social image he carries of himself. That is, he may be helped to see himself objectively, as I pointed out in rehearsal problems. He will shed, under careful creative guidance, the chrysallis that binds him to himself, into greater creative freedom and expression. Whether his handicap is physical, mental or emotional maladjustment, you, as his creative leader, can find his highest level of performance. And if you are creative yourself, you will not hedge him in by preconceived ideas, but estimate his growth by opening wider and wider the doors. What he can take, he will.

In no other field, perhaps, is this so possible. For dramatics is not only an art, it is a slice of life lived by the actors.

In regard to the second point, of yourself seeing the play as a whole by which each student may come to his own fulfilment, therein lies one of the greatest sources of delight. The creative teacher of dramatics will not think in terms of the finished unit, artistically, but as a composite of unexplored personalities for which she is trying to find a plan of creative development. Remembering that "the vision of one man lends not its wings to another man" you must plan so that not only the brilliant student may forge ahead but that your most timid and handicapped child may grow in stature as far as he is capable of going. To insure this, do not be too quick to arrive at a decision yourself. Creative teaching, in its deepest meaning, neither permits the brilliant to be sacrificed to the lesser mind, nor the other way around. And you, the dramatics teacher, have an opportunity to afford development to all.

The third point, that of inspiring each student to work with belief in himself, is the most fundamental. The results are far-reaching, because you give him a workable philosophy. If he has belief in his own unique capacity, whatever its nature or degree, he can make it function for him in life. There are two aspects of this belief worth considering. He obtains some measure of artistic satisfaction that gives him confidence in his *own* creative process. At the same time this belief carries over into his pattern of daily thinking and enables him to be a better-adjusted person. To go back again to the feeble-minded (because we have for so long thought of them as incapable of doing *normal* things) I will give another illustration. A child of very low intelligence wished to be the May Queen. She had no physical attributes that were suitable, on the contrary she was outstandingly ugly. However, she was permitted to act the part. As a result she learned a few fundamentals of movement that, in her case, were valuable to her own development, and she had the great social satisfaction of feeling like other people! We are prone to forget that emotion is not a matter of intellect. That child had an inspirational creative experience.

141

Moreover, students inspired to a belief in their own capacities carry that away into other relationships. Such a creative teacher has touched immortality; she has passed on the torch of the undying fire.

The word "creative" must be significant beyond any art form. To find your own level of creative work is to have established a way of living. Creative power is the means to draw out of any situation all that is in it, intellectually and otherwise. As applied to a dramatic group we mean by creative: an interchange of ideas, a group experience in dramatic form that results in an art form, or play. Not only is such a dramatic form fluid and constantly growing, but it is also a dramatic participation with an audience. The audience is *life* reacting to us, individually, and as a group. Therefore in teaching any creative play, we must bear in mind the place of the audience. Structure is thought of in the meaning the play must have for those who listen.

The audience is not an outside force listening to your results. You must regard the audience as another part of the creative flow in which actors are imaginatively merged. If the play and audience are two separate entities, then you have failed to function creatively. The play (a creative unit) becomes a living reality only when the audience (another creative unit) becomes a part of its growing. The two together make a created, living form.

The creative teacher, herself, never stops growing. The high degree of creative energy generated by the group, when genuinely developing, gives to her too the unified experience of drawing from the resources of her group. That is one of the most vital differences in the creative method of teaching as compared with the more formal type.

Ideas flow. You may present one idea; two or three children in your group present others, and before you are done there is something evolved that is unlike any one of the original ideas. In the same way the pupil's idea ceases to be his alone, and is a composite of all the creative energy of the group and leader, or teacher. This is the reason for that quality of *aliveness* that is to be found in any creatively-conducted class, or group. In the same way the teacher is renewed. It is a truth that the higher the degree of potential gift, the more necessary is its expression for the integration of the personality. That is one of the fundamental reasons why creative dramatics is more than a study; it is a creative release, regardless of whether there is dramatic talent or not. It brings about a flow of free energy that in turn may indicate other creative capacities.

The creative class is the thinking class, it is the feeling class. If the teacher is using the creative process as a means of awakening her class, even stupid children will be more alert. Personality development results from functioning of the entire organism. Your privilege is to help the children to find out what that *self* is! Carbon copies of individuals in class rooms are all too prevalent.

The creative method of teaching then, may be the source of richer living to both teacher and student. Creative energy, once tapped, has a tendency to flow on, into other channels of living. Creative dramatics is a unique opportunity for the teacher to lead towards constructive thinking and living. The technique is the road of travel; hence, whatever of technique must be learned is the future source of success, of creative teaching and living, alike to you and to your classes—who share with you the sense of unfolding of life.

Appendix

GROUP A

OUTLINE FOR REHEARSALS

ACT ONE
Scene 1: *A Queen's Palace*
1. Examines her jewels.
2. Sends for her maid to admire jewels.
3. Questions maid about her own beauty.
4. Maid almost says Snow White is more beautiful.
5. Asks mirror.
6. Sends for Snow White.
7. Asks mirror the second time.
8. Sends for huntsman.
9. Return of huntsman with heart and tongue.

ACT TWO
Scene 1: *Dwarfs' House*
1. Enter Snow White.
2. Eats food.
3. Finds beds and goes to sleep.
4. Return of the dwarfs.
5. Sit at table. Notice things out of place.
6. Seeking her.
7. Finding of Snow White.
8. She tells her story.
9. Dwarfs warn her not to let anyone in.

Scene 2: *Queen's Palace*
1. Queen discovers that Snow White lives.
2. Sends for the huntsman.
3. Consults mirror.
4. Plans disguise and bodice.

Scene 3: *Dwarfs' House*

1. Queen comes in disguise.
2. Persuades Snow White to let her in.
3. Snow White tries on the girdle.
4. The dwarfs return and find her lying there.
5. She awakes and tells her story.
6. She is again warned.

Scene 4: *Queen's Palace*

1. Queen thinks Snow White is dead.
2. Consults her mirror and finds out Snow White lives.
3. Fixes the poisoned comb.

Scene 5: *Dwarfs' House*

1. Queen comes with the comb.
2. Persuades Snow White to let her in.
3. She puts the comb in Snow White's hair.
4. She escapes.
5. The dwarfs come.
6. Snow White revives and tells her story.

Scene 6: *Queen's Palace*

1. Discovery by the Queen that Snow White still lives.
2. Plans to give the poisoned apple to her.
3. Getting ready.

ACT THREE

Scene 1: *Dwarfs' House*

1. Arrival of the Queen in disguise.
2. Offering of the apple.
3. Division of the apple.
4. Death of Snow White.
5. Return of the dwarfs.
6. Grief of the dwarfs.
7. Prince comes.

8. Snow White awakes.
9. Rejoicing and departure.
10. Arrival of Queen.
11. She dies of rage to find Snow White living.
12. All return and celebrate.

GROUP A BACKGROUNDS

The children were from an organized church group in a good neighborhood. The characters were as follows:

The Queen. Eleven year old Syrian of bright mentality. The family is not a charity case although poor.

Snow White. Ten years of age. Norwegian parentage. Middle class. Average intelligence. A secretive temperament and somewhat shy.

Lisa. (maid-huntsman-dwarf). Eleven years of age. Father is dead. The mother works. Average intelligence.

The Prince. Claims to be ten years of age, but has the physical and sex development of twelve or thirteen. He is in the lower fourth grade, and comes from an average home.

Second lady-in-waiting. Eleven years of age. She comes from a well-to-do family. The child is subnormal to a marked degree, with a deep-rooted emotional complex. A hint of criticism makes her totally unable to do anything. She is tall, overgrown, and lacks co-ordination.

Dwarfs: (1) The dwarf who at the last minute took the part of Snow White, is of German parentage. She comes from a large family of a higher grade laboring class. She is above average intelligence and is nine years old. (2) Of the three remaining dwarfs, one came from a well-to-do family, is well-bred, and bright. She is ten years of age. One of the other two dwarfs is eight years of age and the other is nine. The father is dead and the mother works and keeps roomers. The children are bright, precocious, difficult to discipline, and lack restraint.

147

SETTING AND PROPERTIES

In both group A and B the setting and properties of the play, "Snow White and the Dwarfs" were simplified as much as possible.

The only difference in the performance of A and B was in the use of the curtains.

In group A the play was given in a large room with one end curtained off.

In group B it was possible to use three curtains. This made a change of setting unnecessary. That is, one curtain was used for the back-drop or setting; one for the front of the Dwarf-house, and one for a front curtain. The use of ordinary army blankets for the Dwarf-beds conserved space and effort. The curtains were handled by children at the performance.

The cost of the costumes for Group A was under ten dollars. The children watched the cutting and fitting and did quite a little of the sewing. The tights for the Dwarfs were made from ordinary underclothing and dyed in various colors.

Group B also helped in the sewing of their costumes, but practically everything was made from old material such as: lace curtains, old long-cloth, clown suits (made into dwarf costumes), Santa Claus suit (made into the Prince's outfit) and other odds and ends. This was accomplished by re-dying everything. The entire outfit cost less than five dollars.

REHEARSAL REPORT ON GROUP A

At the first meeting of the little group the story of "Snow White and the Seven Dwarfs" was told. There were only six children present, but we decided to act it out nevertheless.

Certain characteristics common to all children were marked. Namely, that all the children who were most interested wanted to be in all the parts and to dictate all stage setting.

Other characteristics more directly related to fundamental dramatic impulses were:

148

The desire of the children to act out the story completely with little or no regard as to whether that part of the story had any bearing on the rest of the drama.

A distinct tendency toward crude humor. The poisoning by the wicked Queen mother did not strike them as sad, but funny. The child then taking the part of Snow White tended to farce it.

There was also the inclination to bring in material relevant to our age, and not at all to the spirit of the fairy tale.

There was a distinct difference in the freedom of expression among the children. Unrestrained imagination in some tended to change the meaning of the story. Other children were distinctly realistic and were bound by that limitation.

SECOND REHEARSAL

There were six new members at the second meeting. This caused considerable repetition and some confusion. The following very interesting things developed.

The children dropped some of the action that had no bearing on the possible play and yet strung one scene to another with no apparent sense of their relationship. Their feeling was apparently that which early plays suggest—the desire for very detailed action rather than leading from one highlight to another.

There was a distinct growth in the power of the children to build out their characters through dialogue. However, the more prominent feature of this was the introduction of irrelevant material.

There was the same desire to have the stage fully set as before.

Evidence of the movies was very prominent. This was also noted in the interpretation of the character of the Queen mother and her lady-in-waiting.

The children felt a need of variety in setting and action which was not shown at the first meeting. At the first rehearsal they were contented to have the dwarfs do the same thing each time between the Queen's visits. The second time they suggested some variety between them. They took Snow White out for a walk, since

149

it was dangerous for her to go alone. Here their sense of humor resulted in a fight with a bear in the woods.

The Queen was a meek and mild little thing and had, as a lady-in-waiting, an executive and bossy type of youngster. This last child showed a tendency towards repartee and characterization. This is illustrated by the following conversation:

Queen. Go get me a poisoned comb.

Lady. I will not unless you promise me a raise in salary.

Queen. I have no more money.

Lady. All right. I'll leave immediately and I'll go back to work for Snow White. I'll cook better meals for her.

I chose this only because it was very typical of much of the conversation, full of present day allusions. This was very obvious in the wedding, which had every indication of being an up-and-coming fashionable wedding.

Third Rehearsal

There were but six children present, but it was the most interesting meeting we had because there was so much freedom of play. The interest of the children in dialogue greatly increased, and we spent over an hour in doing what might be termed the first scene, as it was only the part where the wicked Queen discovers Snow White as her rival that we rehearsed over and over.

The different children exchanged parts. A certain sameness of interpretation of the wicked Queen was in evidence, but there was a constantly increasing wealth of dialogue. The children reached out for more things to do. They still ran their conversation along the lines of present-day experience. Very little imagination was displayed in getting into the experience of the fairy-feeling. They picked up an interesting bit of action by bringing into the conversation the reason why the Queen hated Snow White, whereas in the first playing a separate scene was devoted to the good Queen. This was the first indication of forming the story.

One very noticeable thing was that the children derived great glee from the extreme crossness of the Queen. One child characterized the Queen as shrewish. One had her haughty and cross, but with much less broad humor. Low comedy however, was quite a noticeable thread. The Queens were very severe to the maids. One Queen smoked. This delighted the children.

Upon hearing the mirror's answer the Queen said: "She is more beautiful, is she? I'll see about that." And after the huntsman took Snow White: "Now, I guess that will be a different story."

The second scene of the dwarfs was not so rich, but was interesting because the dialogue and action were different from the last time. The dwarfs acted with more maturity. The interest did not lag at any time. Some interesting things came to light in variations of development when different children took various parts.

We started in where we had left off—in the house of the dwarfs. Snow White told the dwarfs she had learned to cook, as follows:

"My mother, the Queen, was so cross to her maid that the maid got mad and would not cook, then I followed mother to the kitchen and watched her work."

Whereupon the dwarfs all commented on how beautiful everything looked and how good it tasted.

The dwarfs spoke of how cold it was in the mountains to work.

A funny thing happened when Snow White was discovered in bed asleep when she first came to the house of the dwarfs. The dwarfs told how they had heard of a wicked Queen who had a little daughter whom she hated because she was so beautiful. From that they built a story that really carried from point to point. For when Snow White awoke and told her story the dwarfs said to one another, "Ha! that's what we said." This is the first evidence of plot the children have given. Later when changing characters and starting over, there was evidence of a sense of plot development..

The Queen remained consistently cruel, but there is not so much humor about it. The Queen's hand-maiden created a very nice character, as a resigned type of girl.

The huntsman also was good. At the Queen's command to take Snow White out her lines were, "Yes, fair Queen."

In response to the pleadings of Snow White, the huntsman said, "I haven't the heart to kill you. What shall I do?" He then brought back the tongue and heart of a boar that the Queen put in her safe. This is irrelevant and incongruous.

The children always seem to want to finish whatever action is started.

In the house of the Dwarfs at this time the dwarfs did not immediately see Snow White. They did the following: tasted the food; made the beds; made the following remarks *Finger prints* on the table (suspense). Must be someone in the house; let's find her—Here she is! (climax). Do not wake her.

They wonder where she came from. One of the dwarfs tells the story of the magic mirror and wicked mother. One said he had heard in town that the King had bought the mirror for his first wife. When Snow White wakes she verifies the story.

The dwarfs warn Snow White to be very careful. They tell her that her stepmother may come in disguise.

These are pointers given toward a climax. After breakfast the dwarfs wash clothes. They have a wedding with a grand ball, and invite the Queen.

The supposedly subnormal child took the part of the wicked Queen. She got more pride and arrogance into her actions, but there was no new line of thought. She was severe to the maid; called herself beautiful, and ordered beautiful dresses. Beaded gowns have been called for in almost every case, and blue and gold is the favorite color.

In the home of the dwarfs the line of approach was new. In the last rehearsal, one of the dwarfs was said to hear downtown the story of the Queen and the magic mirror. This rehearsal the dwarfs told a story of seeing in the newspaper, while on the street, an advertisement of a little girl lost from the palace. Another dwarf followed this by saying he had known, on his last job, a man who was the huntsman to the Queen and who had offered to get him a job at the palace. But when he, the dwarf, asked for a job, the Queen said he was too dirty. He thought it very silly for the King to ever marry such a person.

The incongruity in this bothered the children not at all. It is a move towards plot and characterization. The dwarfs had three meals a day—very realistic ones. Cake and fresh bread appear regularly. Stew for lunch and plenty of burned tongues for comedy!

Back again with the Queen the first real effort towards disguise was mentioned. The second time the Queen was to appear she wore pillows as a disguise and walked like a fat old woman. One of the dwarfs said that the diamonds in the comb were paste anyhow. This time the Queen got her poisoned articles ready without the knowledge of the maid.

Fifth Rehearsal

The first movement towards making a real play was made at this meeting. The children decided that certain things would have to be "told" in the play, such as:

1. Who the Queen was.
2. That the Queen had a daughter.
3. Where all this happened.
4. The following things about the different characters:
   a. Queen—selfish, wicked, cruel, jealous, proud, vain, and rich.
   b. Maid—kind and sympathetic.

There was nothing like as much free play as there had been. They showed a tendency to repeat themselves without much real spontaneity. The Queen really created a character of harshness, but not at all with any imaginative idea of fairy-play.

Sixth Rehearsal

There were ten children present at this meeting and the greatest creative freedom of any time was enjoyed.

The first act followed about the same lines. The Queen admired her jewels, called the maid for a dress and put on her crown. The only new thing was that in questioning the mirror she pretended not to understand or believe and repeated the question growing more angry the second time. Suspense movement.

The scene in the house of the dwarfs showed a big advance in originality. To help the children we let the dwarfs choose such different types as the bragger, the one that hears all the news, the greedy one, the kind dwarf, an old one. When they came home from work they sat down at the table as usual, found things wrong with their food—then saw a finger spot on the table cloth, from which they concluded someone must be there. Then, the dwarf who hears all the news, told how he had heard the Queen's daughter had run away. So they seek for someone. The "naughty" dwarf found Snow White. The braggart, a cunning little eight year old Italian, said, "I don't see why she didn't lie in my bed—it's the best." The "newsy" one said, "I told you so." Then one of the children said, "she is in my bed, may I sleep with you." (This to the greedy one) "No! Certainly not, I want my bed to myself!" yelled the greedy dwarf. The noise woke Snow White who then told her story. The dwarfs chimed in according to character. At this point we stopped acting and went downstairs to design costumes.

This meeting was disappointing after the interest shown the week before. Once a week allows too much to come between, a daily rehearsal is far better. The Queen again admired her jewels and her money. Spoke again of her wonderful mirror, and wondered if she remained the most beautiful person in the world. She sent for her lady-in-waiting to show off her gown. This part is taken by a child supposedly defective and who does definitely lack co-ordination. The Queen expects her admiration. Then the Queen sends for Snow White to see if she is indeed beautiful. The child taking the part of the Queen has a tendency to pantomime rather than talk. A plot step is indicated when the Queen said, after dismissing Snow White, "It couldn't be! I have it! I'll ask the mirror." This is the first time she has asked the mirror twice. Receiving both times the same answer she thinks, "What can I do now? I'll send for the huntsman to take Snow White and kill her." After this decision she seemed to be happy.

At this meeting we worked on suspense and movements and groupings.

Act One (In the Queen's Room): The Queen is found admiring her jewels, gown, and hair. She called in the maid to admire her beauty. Then she sent for Snow White to admire her. After Snow White left, the Queen took out her golden crown and placing it upon her head, asked the mirror if she were not more beautiful than Snow White. Receiving a negative answer the second time she said, "Even my crown doesn't help; I will kill her! I shall call the huntsman." She offered the huntsman a reward for killing Snow White. When he remonstrated she told him to obey or lose his head. The scene closed with the return of the huntsman with the heart and tongue of the boar. He requested his reward.

Act Two (House of the dwarfs): Snow White comes in, tries all the food, then all the beds, and falls asleep. The dwarfs enter, light their candles, sit down at the table. Here suspense must lead directly towards the climax. The first climax will be finding Snow White. Therefore in order to have the meal interesting, it must lead to Snow White.

The dwarfs find things out of place, finger marks and so on as before. One dwarf in getting food at the fireplace almost finds Snow White. At last they decide a search must be made. When they find her, all sit around the fireplace and she tells them her story. Some of them want her to stay. The greedy one thinks that with Snow White in the house they could all have better food. The grumbly one does not want her.

There must be motivation to make these dwarfs like her. After warning her they go to bed.

Act Two (Queen's Palace): In this scene the Queen is questioning the mirror and finding out that Snow White lives. She prepares the bodice.

Act Three (Dwarfs' House): Snow White is busy at work. The Queen comes in disguise, peeks through the window, holds up the bodice and tempts Snow White. Suspense is worked up by making the temptation stronger and stronger until Snow White yields. Then after she lets the Queen put the girdle on her, suspense is again sustained by the Queen allowing time before the girdle affects Snow White. This was well done with the little Queen pretending to tighten the girdle until at last Snow White lay apparently dead. Then the dwarfs return and find her dead. They try to lift her up and see what is the matter. One dwarf discovers the girdle and says, "What is this?" Snow White begins to remember—"Whose is it? It must be the Queenn's because it so gorgeous. How did she look? How did she put the girdle on?"

Snow White is warned again.

COMMENTS

From this point on to the presentation of the drama there was a sustained upward movement. I have used this group as my illustration for several reasons. First, they were difficult and hence a teacher can see the possibilities. Also because it is the only experiment where I kept a record of exactly what happened. Other groups have had larger numbers but they have also had the advantage of more frequent rehearsals and more experience on my part. The Snow White group was the first one I carried out. I want to point out that in all coaching of this type one grows with the creative experience.

GROUP A—VERBATIM DIALOGUE

Queen. I guess I'll get ready for the ball. I'll put on my crown and my jewels. I'll call Lisa—Lisa, Lisa   (*louder*) Lisa! Where can she be?

Lisa. What is it your majesty?

Queen. Why did you not come when I called you?

Lisa. I did not hear you, my Queen.

Queen. You come when I call.

Lisa. I surely would have, Queen, if I had heard you.

Queen. Go get my gold dress.

Lisa. Yes, your majesty.

Queen. I am so beautiful. I will be the most beautiful person at the ball. I'll ask my mirror that the old witch gave me seven years ago. Mirror on the wall, who is the fairest of us all?

Mirror. Thou wert the fairest, Oh my Queen, but Snow White is fairer far I mean.

Queen. Snow White—I will not have it. I shall call Lisa and get her advice. Lisa!

Lisa. Yes, my Queen.

Queen. Do you not think I am beautiful? Which is more beautiful Snow White or me?

Lisa. Snow—Oh, I mean, you are more beautiful than she is.

Queen. Why didn't you say so then? Go and bring Snow White.

Lisa. Yes, your majesty (*exit*).

Queen. We'll see about this.

(*Enter* LISA *with* SNOW WHITE—*bows*)

Queen. Snow White, you are not to go to the ball tonight. I will not have it.

Snow White. Why not, mother?

Queen. Because I will not be seen with you. . . . Take her away. (*exit*)

Queen. They shall not say she is beautiful. I'll ask the mirror again. It has always told me the truth.

> Mirror, mirror on the wall,
> Who is fairest of us all?

Mirror. Thou wert the fairest
> Oh, my Queen
> But Snow White is fairer
> Far I mean.

Queen. I won't have it. Let me think. I won't have it. I'll poison her or something. Huntsman, huntsman, come here. (*Enter huntsman*)

Huntsman. Here I am, Queen.

Queen. Will you do something for me?

Huntsman. I will do anything you want, fair Queen.

Queen. Then I want you to take Snow White into the forest and kill her, and bring me her heart and her tongue and you shall have a reward.

Huntsman. I could not do that, oh Queen. She is so beautiful.

Queen. You said you'd do anything I asked you. She is not so beautiful as I, is she? Go or your own head shall be the forfeit.

Huntsman. Not any more beautiful, Queen, but I cannot kill her. I'd rather you took my life.

Queen. I am the Queen. You shall do as I say.

Huntsman. (*Smiling to himself*) Very well, your majesty.

Queen. Go. (*exit*) I guess now I'll be most beautiful. I'd like to know what the huntsman meant by smiling.

Huntsman. (*returning*) Here is the heart and the tongue, Queen.

Queen. Put it over there. Did you have a hard time getting rid of her?

Huntsman. No, she did not struggle at all, Queen. Where is my reward?

Queen. Here it is, now go. (*exit*) There. Snow White will never bother me again. I am most beautiful.

Act Two—(Dwarf House)

Snow White. Oh let me in—Let me in quick! Oh, I'm so glad I'm away from that ugly huntsman. Oh isn't this nice? Five little places to eat. I guess I'll sit down here. Mercy, this is sour! Oh, this is just right. I wonder who could live here—things are so tiny. (*sees beds*) Oh aren't these sweet—I think I will go to bed, I'm so tired.

(*Enter Dwarfs*)

Dwarf. I am so tired.

2nd Dwarf. I am so hungry.

3rd Dwarf. I am so glad to be home.

4th Dwarf. I wish I never had to get up from this chair again.

1st Dwarf. What are these big foot prints?

5th Dwarf. Oh, they're nothing.

2nd Dwarf. Somebody's been here.

3rd Dwarf. My, but there is something! Somebody must be here.

4th Dwarf. Shall we follow them?

1st Dwarf. No, I am going to finish my supper.

2nd Dwarf. I am going to follow them. They go around this chair.

3rd Dwarf. Into this bed.

All. Oh, how beautiful. (*seeing* SNOW WHITE)

1st Dwarf. Well, I might as well see.

4th Dwarf. Shall we wake her?

All. Let's.

Snow White. Oh! Who are you?

Dwarfs. We are little dwarfs. We will not harm you.

Snow White. Goodness! How small you are.

Dwarfs. We do not grow any bigger.

Snow White. I am so afraid the hunstman will catch me.

Dwarfs. What is your name?

Snow White. Snow White.

Dwarf. That is good. You may sit in my chair, Snow White. I have had my supper.

Snow White. All right. Thank you. When I came in this little house, it is so tiny, I was afraid the huntsman would be chasing me.

Dwarf. Now, Snow White, if you will not let anyone in this house and if you will do all the cooking and sewing and everything, you can stay here.

Snow White. Oh that will be so beautiful, if I can stay here.

All Dwarfs. Yes—surely.

159

Snow White. Oh that will be fine.

Dwarfs. Let us dance. Come and join the dance Snow White. (*exit dwarfs*) Good-bye Snow White!

Scene 2 (Queens Palace)

Page. We are back at the Queen's Palace.

Queen. Now that I am rid of Snow White, I think I will look into my magic mirror.

> "Mirror, mirror on the wall,
> Who is fairest of us all?"

Mirror. Thou wert the fairest, Oh Queen, but Snow White is the fairest of all. She lives across the hill in the house of the seven Dwarfs.

Queen. Snow White! I thought she was dead! That huntsman has deceived me! What shall I do? I must think of a way to get rid of Snow White. I have it. I shall go to the dwarfs' home and strangle her to death with one of my pretty bodices. I will go in disguise. I will go in the disguise of an old woman. Maid, bring me one of my pretty girdles. Hurry! (*Maid with clothes*) I will go into my chamber and dress.

Scene 3

Snow White. I wonder when the dwarfs will be home. (*Knocking at the door*) Is someone at the door? Who's there?

Queen. It is only a poor old lady selling wares.

Snow White. Oh but I must not let anyone in.

Queen. You must. I have beautiful girdles to show you. (*Shows it through the window*).

Snow White. Oh, it is beautiful, but I must not let anyone in the house. I am sorry.

Queen. But I shall not harm you.

Snow White. All right. You may come in. I wonder if the dwarfs will care.

Queen. You do not need to tell them.

Snow White. Oh let's see it. How beautiful.

Queen. Do you want me to try it on you?

Snow White. Oh, yes.

Queen. I have one, but it isn't so expensive like this one. I am too poor to buy girdles.

Snow White. Yes. It looks nice. How beautiful it is. Oh, do not pull it so tight.

Queen. You can walk around with it on. It isn't tight enough.

Snow White. Yes it is.

Queen. I will pull it tighter.

Snow White. Not so tight.

Queen. That is nothing.

Snow White. Oh! Oh! Stop! Oh! Dwarfs!

Queen. Bad child! How am I to get out? (*exit*)

(*Enter Dwarfs*)

Dwarfs. I thought I heard someone calling us. Where is Snow White? We must find her. Do you want a light? Oh, Snow White! (*Seeing her*) What is on her? Isn't it beautiful? This looks like some of the Queen's work.

Snow White. Water!

Dwarfs. We told you not to let anyone in . . . Yes, we told you.

Snow White. It was just an old woman. I did not think you would mind.

Dwarfs. But we do mind. We do not want you to be killed.

Snow White. She was very old, I couldn't turn her down. She was so poor, and she had such a beautiful girdle.

Dwarf. But you did not know, it might have been the Queen in disguise.

Snow White. Oh never—She was only a poor old lady—Oh no. She was so old and all dressed in rags and she wanted to sell me this lovely girdle and I let her in. She was going to stay awhile, but she went away.

Dwarfs. She went away because she was guilty. She ran because you called us.

Snow White. Here is some food.

Dwarfs. Thank you Snow White. I am so glad she was not killed. I am finished (*Taking off Snow White's girdle*)

Snow White. Oh that was so tight around me I couldn't breathe.

Dwarfs. Snow White, do not ever let anyone in the house again. Isn't it time we went to bed?

Snow White. Yes, it is.

Dwarfs. Thank you for the lovely supper. Thank you Snow White.

Scene 4 (Queen's Palace)

Queen. What a narrow escape I had! What if those dwarfs had seen me. I do not care. I strangled Snow White and I think she is dead now. I will go and consult my magic mirror.

  Mirror, mirror, etc. . . .

Queen. Snow White! I thought she was dead . . . and I killed her with my own hands too. I must think of a different plan. I've got it! Maid, bring me a different disguise and bring me one of my ivory combs and a bottle of poison. I'll fix her—I will go to Snow White's house once more and we'll see! We'll see if she lives again. . . . The dwarfs must have brought her back to life. Maybe they discovered the girdle. . . . I wish that maid would hurry!

(*Enter* Maid)

Maid. Wouldn't you like to have me comb your hair . . .

Queen. Oh no. I will do it myself. Now. I'll fix her this time. I'll fix this so it will stick to Snow White's hair—there. Now to go to Snow White's house and put an end to her.

Scene 5 (Dwarfs' House)

Snow White. We are back at the house of the dwarfs.

Snow White. (*Knocking at the door is heard*) Who's there? Who's there?

Queen. Only a poor old lady. I am selling combs.

Snow White. How beautiful. . . . But I cannot let you in.

Queen. Oh, nobody would harm you, you are too beautiful.

Snow White. The dwarfs said not to let anyone in because last time I found a lot of harm.

Queen. What did she do?

Snow White. She nearly killed me.

Queen. But I won't harm you—You are too beautiful.

Snow White. Oh, how pretty! May I comb your hair first?

Queen. Oh no. I will comb your hair, and then you will comb mine.

Snow White. But wait! It is all wet. How funny it is. Oh, I am so dizzy—Oh take it out of my hair, quick—Oh Dwarfs, Dwarfs! (*Enter the dwarfs*)

Dwarfs. Did I hear someone calling us again? And Snow White is not here. Oh Snow White! Snow White! The child will never learn not to let anyone in. Oh, a comb! It must be poison. Let it down, do you want to get poisoned too? Snow White, we told you. You should remember what we tell you.

Snow White. What was that?

Dwarfs. You had a comb in your hair, Snow White.

Snow White. Somebody came here and started combing my hair.

Dwarfs. Why did you let them in? The Queen, Snow White.

Snow White. I know, but this lady looked kind.

Dwarfs. People look to be kind, Snow White, but they are not. Let us go and have our supper. Oh, how lovely. How good!

Snow White. I made it this morning.

Dwarfs. You did! Well, we have to go back to work again. Oh, I wish we did not have to work. Now Snow White, this time remember not to let anyone come in. Goodbye, remember do not let anyone come in.

SCENE 6 (Queen's Palace)

Queen. There now, Snow White is surely dead after I poisoned her. I knew the Huntsman deceived me and one of the guards has banished him from the kingdom and if I ever see him

163

again he shall surely die. I think I shall look into my magic mirror, Mirror, mirror etc. Snow White again! I thought she was dead. What shall I do? I must do something. I suppose I shall have to poison her again. I have a plan. I can give her a poisoned apple. I will poison half the apple, then to make her eat it, I will eat the half that isn't poisoned. . . . I think that will be a good idea. Maid, bring me a bottle of poison and bring me an apple. Hurry! Also a knife. Now I'll fix her. I suppose I'll have to go to Snow White's house again though. I shall do anything to get her dead. (*Enter* MAID)

Maid. Wouldn't you like me to pare it for you?

Queen. No. That is all right. . . . There now. . . . Now I will go to Snow White's house and keep on going until I have her dead.

ACT THREE (Dwarfs' House)

Snow White. I wonder how soon the dwarfs will be home. (*Knocking again heard*) Goodness, who's there?

Queen. I am just a lady selling apples.

Snow White. Oh, but I must not let anyone in.

Queen. Why? I wouldn't do you any harm.

Snow White. But the dwarfs said not to let anyone in.

Queen. Oh, this is the house of the dwarfs I've heard so much about? Well, I am the dwarfs' friend but they wouldn't remember me. I knew them a year ago.

Snow White. You know the dwarfs?

Queen. Surely.

Snow White. Oh then you can come in. . . . What have you?

Queen. I have apples. If you will give me a bit of tea, I shall give you half.

Snow White. Oh, sure. Sit right down here—No, here. Here I will give you something.

Queen. There, now I shall cut this in half.

Snow White. Oh thank you—(*eats it*) Oh Dwarfs!

164

Queen. Now where shall I go? (*exit*) (*Hides behind the curtain.*)

(*Enter dwarfs*)

Dwarfs. Oh did we hear somebody calling us again?

I thought we did.

Snow White!

Look at the apple!

Snow White!

Oh, she is dead.

Has she a comb?

Has she a bodice?

She has nothing.

Oh, she took a bite of the apple.

Oh Snow White.

Oh she will never come to life again.

Snow White.

She's dead, brother.

Yes, she's dead.

Yes. (*Knocking at the door*)

Who's that?

(*Enter the* PRINCE)

Who are you?

Prince. I am a Prince.

Dwarfs. Oh! Our little sister is dead!

Prince. My goodness! Can I see her? Oh how beautiful!

Dwarf. Is she not beautiful?

Prince. She is the most beautiful one I have ever seen. Could I have her?

Dwarf. No! No!

All. No! No! She is so beautiful.

Prince. What do you do?

Dwarfs. We work in the mountains.

We can't see her as much as he can.

He can sit by her all day watching her.

Shall we give her up?

165

Oh can we come and see her?
What shall you do with her?

Prince. I shall put her in a glass cage. Snow White!

Snow White. (*To the* PRINCE) Who are you?

Prince. I am a Prince and you belong to me now.

Snow White. Oh no, I belong to the dwarfs.

Prince. The dwarfs gave you to me.

Snow White. Oh no.

Dwarfs. We thought you were dead and gave you up.

Snow White. All right. (*All go out—enter the Queen*)

Queen. The mirror told me that Snow White was the bride of a Prince. . . . I have come to see. I must see them with my own eyes to believe it. . . . Snow White isn't here. Here they come —OH! I shall die of anger—(*She falls dead*)

Dwarfs. What's that?
Oh! The Queen.
She is dead.

All. HURRAH!

GROUP B

FAMILY BACKGROUND

The children were in a Day Nursery in connection with Hull House. Their ages were eight to eleven years.

Queen. Eleven years of age. Born in Sicily and brought to America at the age of six. The father deserted the mother. The family number eight children, four of whom live with the mother and four with the father. The mother is odd, but is a good housekeeper and good to the children. The child is mentally bright.

Snow White. Age nine, of German parentage. The father and mother both work. The father earns only eighteen dollars a week. The family is extremely poor. There are six children and they all live together in a two room shack. Two of the sisters took parts as dwarfs—All were of dull intelligence.

166

Appendix — Group B

Huntsman (also part as dwarf).   Eleven years of age. She was born in Italy. Her intelligence was about that of the average seven year old child. She was called a high grade moron. She was a very sensitive child and possessed a marked inferiority feeling. She has deep love for dramatics. The mother is dead and the father takes care of the three little girls and is kind to them.

Letitia (also the Prince).   She is eleven years of age with superior intelligence and excellent poise.

First Dwarf.   She is eight years of age. She came from Italy when a baby; is subnormal. The mother is inadequate, twice divorced, and has gone down the scale steadily. The house is dirty and conditions are unclean.

OUTLINE

Deviation from the outline as it was perfected at the final rehearsal is explained under the main discussion.

ACT ONE

1. Queen is examining jewels.
2. Sends maid for more jewels.
3. Asks mirror—refuses to believe.
4. Sends for maid to admire her.
5. Wants to see Snow White.
6. Asks mirror second time.
7. Sends for huntsman.
8. Return of huntsman.

ACT TWO—*Scene 1*

1. Snow White comes, tired and hungry.
2. Eats—motive for dwarfs to find something wrong with the table on their return (Three Bears).
3. Falls asleep.

Scene 2

1. Return of the dwarfs.
2. Sit at table.

3. Discover things wrong.
4. Seek Snow White.
5. Find her—front center.
6. Snow White's story.
7. Warning of the dwarfs.
8. Departure of dwarfs.

Scene 3

1. Queen comes.
2. Calls, "Wares."
3. Shows wares in window.
4. Snow White doing dishes.
5. At first refuses—finally yields—lets Queen in.
6. Tries on bodice.

Scene 4

1. Cook comes first.
2. Finds Snow White.
3. Calls brothers.
4. All bend over Snow White—see bodice.
5. Snow White tells story about old woman.
6. Dwarfs warn her, then go.

Scene 5

1. Queen is seen watching through window as Dwarfs leave.
2. Queen shows comb.
3. Snow White slow to let her in—getting ready to go to market.
4. Lets her in to see her.
5. Queen puts comb in Snow White's hair.
6. Snow White falls.

Scene 6

1. One dwarf comes back.
2. Finds note about going to market.

3. Starts to fix tables.
4. Stumbles over Snow White.
5. All dwarfs come.
6. Dwarfs repeat warning.
7. All go to bed.

Act Three—*Scene* 1, Queen's Room

1. Queen speaks to mirror.
2. Calls huntsman for reprimand.
3. Calls for maid for the disguise.
4. Apple.

Scene 2, House of the Dwarfs

1. Queen appears at window.
2. Persuasion.
3. Division of apple.
4. Death of Snow White.
5. Return of dwarfs.
6. Weeping.
7. Cover Snow White.
8. Prince arrives.
9. Wedding.

REHEARSALS

At first timidity interfered greatly with creative work. After running through the play and being prompted by suggestions they began to play with it somewhat. The only way in which there was a marked resemblance to the other group was in the following:

Getting low comedy into the play—usually through irrelevant material.

The children also made a great deal of the eating in the dwarfs' house and wanted to get in every detail.

There was less tendency on the part of the children to have

things matter-of-fact and true to today's life. There was more imagination.

The Queen at this meeting of Group B did one thing which was quite different from the other children. She had her magic mirror brought to her by her hand-maiden instead of having it in the room. These children, as in Group A, also brought the heart and tongue of the boar back.

In the house of the dwarfs there was an entirely new trend of imagination. When the dwarfs found Snow White in their house she described the palace where she had lived. She said it had a high steeple and was up high on a hill. At the table there was a decided tendency towards horseplay and the bringing in of irrelevant material. When they slept they snored loudly. One dwarf only shaved upon arising.

When the dwarfs went to work they warned Snow White about allowing anyone to enter. After her stepmother came and succeeded in tieing the bodice about her, an entirely original and new turn was taken in this group.

The dwarfs, upon hearing her story, declared they had passed the palace on the way to the mountains to work and one of them had heard the Queen through the window asking the mirror who was most beautiful now. He said also that he met a man from the palace who was advertising to see where Snow White was.

Then Snow White decided that next time her mother came she would try to disguise her voice and pretend to be a dwarf. If anyone tried to sell her anything she would ask so many questions that they would get tired and leave.

There was decided low comedy in this scene when enacted. Unguided, they would have allowed it to run away with them. As it was, when the dwarfs came home and found the comb in her hair, they warned her that it would be her own fault if she was killed. They wanted to leave a dwarf to take care of her, but saw for themselves that it would not work out.

When Snow White died this time some of the dwarfs wept, but there was again an almost irresistable desire to farce it. The wedding was much more formal and conducted with much less horseplay than in Group A.

The new points in development were the discarding of low comedy in favor of more real drama. Characterization began to appear in the different dwarfs. Material was well carried over from one rehearsal to another. The Queen made an exciting thing of her preparations for Snow White's death and fussed over her disguise—using suspense well. When she came down the street selling her wares it was easy to recognize the Halsted peddler. Snow White was the typical Italian peasant mother—another local-color touch was the visit of the dwarfs to the fortune teller to find out if the Queen was still seeking Snow White. The story element decidedly dominates in these plays.

GROUP B—VERBATIM DIALOGUE

CHARACTERS: Queen, Snow White, Letitia, Dwarfs, Prince, Huntsman.

ACT ONE—*Scene 1*

Queen. Why, how beautiful I look—with my pretty rose cheeks and bright eyes. I am more beautiful than snow. (*To lady in waiting*) Fix my train. (*Again admiring self*) My rosy cheeks are just like a big rose. I am more beautiful than Snow White. (*To lady in waiting*) How long you are. I should like to see Snow White in this room.

Letitia. Yes, your Honor.

(*Enter Snow White*)

Queen. Snow White, sit down. Now Snow White, you are more beautiful than I. You are going to be locked up in a big dark room.

Snow White. Oh, Mother, don't lock me in a dark room. What did I do to you?

Queen. You shall be locked up and never see daylight.

Snow White. What did I do?

171

Queen. Letitia, take her out. (*to self*) Now I shall see who is more beautiful.

Mirror, mirror on the wall
Who is fairer than us all?

Mirror. Thou O Queen, art wondrous fair,
But Snow White in the Glen
Is a thousand times more fair.

Queen. Snow White again. She is the ugliest girl I ever have seen. Letitia, get the huntsman as quickly as you can.

Letitia. Huntsman, huntsman, oh huntsman.

Huntsman. Here I am.

Queen. Huntsman, I will tell you something and it is that you shall take Snow White out into the woods and bring me her head.

Huntsman. Oh no, I do not want to.

Queen. You shall. I will give you a reward.

Huntsman. But Snow White is a beautiful girl.

Queen. You shall. I will give you a reward.

Huntsman. Oh, no, I do not want to.

Queen. You shall get your head chopped off if you do not bring her in the wood and kill her. (*Exit all but the Queen*) Now that Snow White is killed I am more beautiful than any other lady in the land. (*Calls Letitia*) Letitia, tell me who is more beautiful than I.

Letitia. My mistress, you are beautiful, but I think Snow White is more beautifuler.

Queen. She is not. You must not be my lady in waiting anymore.

Letitia. Please Queen, I did not mean to say it.

Queen. I will forgive you this time but never insult me again.

Scene 2. (House of the dwarfs)

Snow White. Oh, what a beautiful little house with five little chairs and five little bowls and five little beds. Oh, how hungry I am. I will eat. This is too hot. This is too cold. This is very, very hot. This is too cold. This is very, very hot. This is just right. I will eat. Oh, how tired I am. I will go to bed. This is too high. This is too low. This is too hard. This is too soft. This is too downy. This is just right. I will sleep (*trying beds*).

(*Enter dwarfs.*)

First Dwarf. Oh, how tired I am. I have been digging all day.

Second Dwarf. So have I.

All. So have I.

First Dwarf. I am so hungry, I will eat.

Second Dwarf. But brother, you must cook first.

Third Dwarf. It has been very hot for digging.

Fourth Dwarf. Brother, hurry we are hungry.

Fifth Dwarf. Oh, but the table is disorderly.

Second Dwarf. Someone has been using my spoon.

Third Dwarf. Someone threw my fork on the floor and ate my pudding.

Fourth Dwarf. Someone used my knife.

All. Somebody has been in this house.

Second Dwarf. All I want is to eat. I'm hungry.

First Dwarf. We shall look. There is no one under this table.

Third Dwarf. Let us look under the beds.

First Dwarf. What a beautiful girl! Isn't she beautiful.

Third Dwarf. With light hair and a pretty dress on.

Fourth Dwarf. I hope she will stay with us. Wake her, brother.

Snow White. (*waking*) Oh, where am I?

All. You are in the dwarfs' house.

Snow White. But how did I get there?

Dwarfs. Would you like to sit down on the floor and tell us?

Snow White. My mother she is a rich woman. She chased me away from her palace and told the huntsman to kill me, but he let me free.

First Dwarf. What is your name?

Snow White. My name is Snow White.

Second Dwarf. What does the huntsman do?

Snow White. He takes the little boys and girls into the woods and tries to kill them.

Third Dwarf. What does a palace look like?

Snow White. It is on a high hill and has a steeple.

Fourth Dwarf. Why did she turn you out of the house?

Snow White. Because she said I was beautifuler than she.

Fifth Dwarf. You will stay with us. We have five beds and we will have another. It is time; brothers, let us go. Now, don't open the door for anyone.

Scene 3

Snow White. (*Tidying up the place*)

Old Lady. (*Knocking*) Little girl, little girl, what are you doing?

Snow White. I am sweeping. What do you want?

Old Lady. I would like to make you buy a bodice, the prettiest one.

Snow White. I do not want to buy any bodice.

Old Lady. I will not hurt you, let me in.

Snow White. All right, you may come in.

Old Lady. Open the door quickly.

Snow White. But what do you want? How much does it cost?

Old Lady. Fifty cents. Here let me try it on you. It is the the prettiest bodice you ever have seen. Go and get the money. What is your name? Oh, let me fix it a little better. (*Squeezes* Snow White *until she falls*) Aha! She is dead and I am more beautiful than Snow White. (*Leaves*) (*Enter Dwarf*)

Dwarf. Oh, this gold is very heavy. I will put it down. Where can the little maid be? I will look for her. Oh! Here she is. She is dead. I will run and call my brothers. Brothers, brothers, Snow White is lying on the floor. (*Enter dwarfs*)

Dwarfs. Lying on the floor? Where is she?

All. She is dead.

Fifth Dwarf. I told you to leave the door closed and you

174

would not mind me. It must have been her wicked mother. It is a Queen's bodice. Let us put it away for she might put it on again and fall dead. Get up Snow White, and tell us about it. Snow White, you are too beautiful to be dead.

Snow White. An old lady came in this house and she said, "Do you want to buy a bodice?"

First Dwarf. Why did you not leave the door closed when we told you?

Snow White. She said it was beautiful.

First Dwarf. Now, be careful and leave the door closed when we say so.

Snow White. All right.

Dwarfs. Now we shall go to work again. Snow White, always let the door shut.

Snow White. I will get through my sweeping.

Old Lady. (*Knocking*) Why are you so sad? Don't be sad but let me in and I will sell you a beautiful comb.

Snow White. The dwarfs have one.

Old Lady. Oh, no they haven't. Why are you so sad, tell me.

Snow White. All right you may come in, and I will tell you. Sit down.

Old Lady. Look at this beautiful comb and I have only this one left. I will sell it because I want to support my living.

Snow White. A woman came yesterday and she said to me, "I want you to see a bodice."

Old Lady. What is a bodice?

Snow White. It is a black thing to put on your stomach.

Old Lady. But this comb for your beautiful hair. Let me comb it. (*Stabs* Snow White *with comb*) Ha, she is dead and no one will know anything about it. (Snow White *sits in sleeping position*)

(*Enter Dwarfs*)

First Dwarf. How tired I am. Look at Snow White. She must be asleep, Call her.

Second Dwarf. Isn't she beautiful?

175

Third Dwarf. How did she get that? She must have had to buy it. (*Comb*)

First Dwarf. Nobody would come in. (*Pulls comb out and* SNOW WHITE *sits up*)

All. Snow White, you have come to us. We are so glad. Sit down and tell us your story.

Snow White. An old lady came to me again. She said do you want to buy a beautiful comb and I said the dwarfs have one.

First Dwarf. You said you would not let anybody else in. This chair is moved and someone must have been here and you gave her food.

Snow White. She said she was hungry.

Second Dwarf. Well, I will not hear any more. I am so tired. I have dug gold today.

Scene 4 (Queen's Palace)

Letitia. Queen, I found your gorgeous gown on a chair. Why did you take it off?

Queen. I visited some of my friends. They are so poor I felt ashamed to wear my fine clothes. I will not put it on. Call the huntsman as quickly as you can. Now the huntsman he is a very fine man but he does not do anything I tell him. He may be ascared to come. Call him once more.

Letitia. Huntsman—huntsman.

Queen. I will call him. HUNTSMAN! Come quickly . . . . you shall be very quick about it. (*Enter* HUNTSMAN)

Huntsman. I did not hear.

Letitia. He went on an errand and I forgot to tell you.

Queen. How is Snow White getting along?

Huntsman. Snow White is dead.

Queen. She is not. I went over to her house twice. You shall not be alive. You shall take Snow White's place and your head shall be chopped off.

Huntsman. Oh, I do not want my head chopped off.

Queen. Letitia, bring some man to take his head off.

Huntsman. Please don't.

Queen. I will forgive you this time but never come to my palace again. Now I shall think. What must I do? I will tell the mirror which is most beautiful.

> Mirror, mirror, on the wall,
> Who is fairer than us all?

Mirror. Thou, O Queen, art wondrous fair
> But Snow White in the glen
> With the seven little men
> Is a thousand times more fair.

Queen. What must I do? I have it. Go out into the garden and get me the prettiest apple you can find.

Letitia. What do you want with an apple?

Queen. I just feel like having an apple today.

Letitia. We have nice things in the kitchen.

Queen. Go — — Get me an apple.

Letitia. O Queen, this is the ripest apple in the garden. Do you want a knife?

Queen. If you wish. Now be gone. (*Cuts apple and puts poison into one half.*) This part is poison. This Snow White shall have and this I shall eat. I shall hurry before Letitia finds me.

Scene 5 (Dwarfs' House)

Snow White. (*Sewing*) I am lonesome for the huntsman and Letitia. I wish they were with me. I am very glad that the huntsman left me free. I wish I could see Letitia and the huntsman.

Old Lady. (*Springing forward*) Who is it you want to see?

Snow White. Oh!

Old Lady. Why are you so frightened? I have the most beautiful apple you have ever seen. It just came from California.

Snow White. I do not want any.

Old Lady. I would like to speak to you. May I sit down? Who are the huntsman and Letitia?

Snow White. Letitia is a maid in the palace

Old Lady. What does she do?

Snow White. She eats and she waits upon the Queen.

Old Lady. Who is the huntsman?

Snow White. I will tell you the story of the huntsman. My mother told me that I was no good; that I should get my head cut off and she told the huntsman to take me into the woods and kill me.

Old Lady. Why, you are the most beautiful girl I ever saw but I shall never think you shall be killed. I am very tired and I should like to make you take a bit of this rosy apple.

Snow White. I don't want it.

Old Lady. Take it. See I am eating half. This apple is the most beautiful apple and I want that you shall taste it. (SNOW WHITE *takes bite and falls over.*)

Queen. You are dead now and you are not beautiful again. Never tell me that story anymore, you ugly, ugly creature. (*Exit*) (*Enter Dwarfs*)

Dwarfs. Snow White, Snow White. She does not answer. What has happened to her? I shall call her again. Snow White. Maybe someone has harmed her. Let us all call her once more. Oh, let us in. (*They enter*) Oh, here she is. She is dead. Our poor little maiden who cooked all the time and did our work. And such a beautiful girl she was. Oh, Snow White, get up, get up. (*All weep*).

Dwarfs. We shall not put her away. We shall keep her forever. (*Knocking at the door*)

Fifth Dwarf. Brother, you are the biggest, you shall go.

Prince. (*Entering*) How dark it is here. Haven't you got any light at all. This is on a mountain. How strange it is. Different from a palace.

First Dwarf. Where did you come from, young man?

Prince. And do you not know I am a Prince?

Second Dwarf. What are you here for?

Prince. I was riding in the forest.

Third Dwarf. Oh, what a beautiful hat. You have a big feather. He shall not laugh. Our beautiful maiden is dead.

Prince. I did not see the maiden. I came to ask if I might stay for the night.

Dwarfs. We have only five beds and one for Snow White.

Prince. Can't you put two chairs together? How pretty she is.

Dwarf. She has come to us about two days ago and she has been harmed and we got her back two times but this time we never shall. What are you walking around about?

Prince. I think she is the Princess I have been looking for.

First Dwarf. What will you give us for her?

Prince. I will give you a horse.

Dwarfs. No we don't want a horse. We want gold.

Prince. I have to work for my gold.

Dwarfs. No we have enough gold.

Prince. I will give you more gold than you ever saw.

Dwarfs. All right. (PRINCE *starts to raise Princess into his arms. Piece of apple falls out of her mouth.*)

Dwarfs. Look what is this? It is a piece of apple. Let us throw it into the fire. Sit down, Snow White and let us hear what you have to tell us. (*To* PRINCE) Do not throw your hat on the floor. (*To* SNOW WHITE) Hurry up, speak up.

Snow White. Three days ago I was harmed, the first day I had a bodice; the second day a comb and now an apple.

All. An apple?

Snow White. The old woman said it was the ripest apple in California.

Dwarfs. Oh, let us go. We want to see your palace.

Snow White. I don't know where it is.

Prince. Now I will take you to my palace and there we shall be married and have a wedding.

Bibliography

BOOKS

Andrews, Gladys. *Creative Rhythmic Movement for Children*. Englewood Cliffs, N. J.: Prentice-Hall, 1954.

Bennett, Rowena. *Creative Plays and Programs for Holidays*. Boston: Plays, Inc., 1966.

Brown, Corrine. *Creative Drama in the Lower School*. New York: Appleton Century-Crofts, 1929.

Brown, Regina. *A Play At Your House*. New York: Ivan Obolensky, Inc., 1962.

Burger, Isabel B. *Creative Play Acting*. New York: A. S. Barnes & Co., 1950.

Byers, Ruth. *Creating Theatre*. San Antonio, 1968.

Chorpenning, Charlotte B. *Twenty One Years with Children's Theatre*. Anchorage, Kentucky: Anchorage Press, 1954.

Cole, Natalie. *The Arts in the Classroom*. New York: The John Day Co., 1940.

Davis, Jed H. and Mary Jane Watkins. *Children's Theatre*. New York: Harper & Brothers, 1960.

Durrell, Donald D. and B. Alice Crossley. *Favorite Plays for Classroom Reading*. Boston, Mass.: Plays, Inc., 1965.

Fisher, Caroline and Hazel G. Robutson. *Children and the Theatre*. London, 1950.

Fitzgerald, Burdette. *Let's Act the Story*. San Francisco: Fearon Publishers, 1957.

————. *World Tales for Creative Dramatics and Storytelling*. Englewood Cliffs, N. J.: Prentice-Hall, 1962.

Haaga, Agnes and Patricia Randles. *Supplementary Materials for Use in Creative Dramatics with Younger Children*. Seattle: University of Washington, 1952.

180

Bibliography

Howard, Vernon. *Acts for Comedy Shows*. New York: Sterling Publishing Co., 1966.

————. *The Complete Book of Children's Theatre*. Garden City: Doubleday & Co., 1969.

Kerman, Gertrude. *Plays and Creative Ways with Children*. Irving-on-the-Hudson, N. Y., Harvey House, 1961.

Kamemman, Sylvia E. *Fifty Plays for Junior Actors*. Boston: Plays, Inc., 1966.

Kissen, Fan. *The Bag of Fire and Other Plays*. Boston: Houghton-Mifflin & Co., 1964.

————. *The Golden Goose and Other Plays*. Boston: Houghton-Mifflin & Co., 1963.

————. *The Straw Ox and Other Plays*. Boston: Houghton-Mifflin & Co., 1964.

Lease, Ruth G. and Geraldine B. Siks. *Creative Dramatics for Home, School, and Community*. New York: Harper & Bros., 1952.

Mearns, Hughes. *Creative Power* (Revised). New York: Dover Publications, 1958.

Reeves, James. *The Peddler's Dream and Other Plays*. New York: E. P. Dutton & Co., 1963.

Sanders, Sandra. *Creating Plays with Children*. New York: Scholastic Book Services, 1970.

Sawyer, Ruth. *The Way of the Storyteller*. New York: The Viking Press, 1942.

Seattle J. Programs, Incorporated. *Children's Theatre Manual*, Anchorage, Kentucky: Anchorage Press, 1951.

Siks, Geraldine B. and Hazel B. Dunnington, *Children's Theatre and Creative Dramatics*. Seattle, Washington: University of Washington Press, 1961.

————. *Creative Dramatics: An Art for Children*. New York: Harper & Bros., 1958.

Slade, Peter. *Child Drama.* London: The University of London Press, 1954.

Smith, Moyne R. *Plays and How to Put them On.* New York: Henry Z. Welch, Inc., 1961.

Ward, Winifred. *Drama with and for Children.* Washington, D. C.: U. S. Government Printing Office, 1960.

———. *Playmaking with Children.* New York: Appleton Century-Crofts, 1957.

———. *Stories to Dramatize.* Anchorage, Kentucky: Children's Theatre Press, 1952.

———. *Theatre for Children.* (Revised) Anchorage, Kentucky: Children's Theatre Press, 1950.

Way, Brian. *Development Through Drama.* London, 1967.

PERIODICALS

Anderson, John E. "Psychological Aspects of Child Audiences," *Educational Theatre Journal,* XX (1950), pp. 285-291.

Ayllon, Maurice and Susan Snyder. "Behavioral Objectives in Creative Dramatics," *Journal of Educational Research,* LXII (1969), pp. 339-355.

Bell, Campton. "The Psychology of the Child Audience," *World Theatre,* II (1952), pp. 23-29.

Brush, Martha. "Report on the Seventh Annual Children's Theatre Conference," *Educational Theatre Journal,* III (1951), pp. 192-197.

Burger, Isabel B. "Creative Dramatics: An Educational Tool," *The Instructor,* LXXIII (1963), pp. 133-136.

Davis, Jed H. "Prospectus for Research in Children's Theatre," *Educational Theatre Journal,* XIII (1961), pp. 274-277.

Engbretson, William E. "Values of Children, How they are Developed," *Childhood Education,* XXXV (1959), pp. 259-264.

Faulkes, Margaret. "Secondary School Drama in Britain," *The Secondary School Theatre,* IX (1970), pp. 4-6, 8, 14.

Bibliography

Gair, Sondra Battist. "Theatre: A Total Art Experience for Children," *Art Education*, XXIII (1970), pp. 29-30.

Gillies, Emily. "Crosses and Knives," *Childhood Education*, May, 1946; April, 1947.

Goldberg, Moses. "An Experiment in Theatre for the Five to Eight Year Olds," *Children's Theatre Review*, XIX (1970), p. 7-11, 18.

Hobgood, Burnet M. "The Concept of Experimental Learning in the Arts," *Educational Theatre Journal*, XXII (1970), pp. 43-52.

Jackson, Eugene R. "Children's Theatre is a Seed: Adult Theatre is the Plant," *Children's Theatre Review*, XIX (1970), pp. 12-14; 31-32.

Karieth, Joseph. "Creative Dramatics as Aid in Developing Creative Thinking Abilities," *Educational Theatre Journal*, XIX, (1970), pp. 301-309.

McSwain, E. T. "The Art Experience in the Development of the Child's Personality," *Educational Theatre Journal*, II (1953), pp. 125-127.

Merow, Erva Loomis. "Every Child on Stage," *The Instructor*, LXXIX (1970), pp. 26-39.

Owen, Hal. "Writing Plays for Children," *California Journal of Elementary Education*, XXV (1957), pp. 146-151.

Popovich, James. "Highlights of the Children's Theatre Conference," *Educational Theatre Journal*, XI (1958), pp. 325-335.

Shaw, Ann M. "A Taxonomical Study of the Nature and Behavioral Objectives of Creative Dramatics," *Educational Theatre Journal*, XXII (1970), pp. 361-372.

Spencer, Sara. "Children's Theatre, Past and Present," *Educational Theatre Journal*, VII (1955), pp. 44-46.

Strawbridge, Edwin. "Do Your Play For Not To the Children," *Recreation*, XLVII (1954), pp. 484-486.

Tucker, JoAnne K. "Movement in Creative Dramatics," *Children's Theatre Conference Newsletter*, XV (1966), pp. 9-12.

Turner, Pearl Ibsen. "Far Better than the Ready-Made Play," *Instructor*, LXXVII (1967), pp. 47ff.

Van Tassel, Wesley, "Differences in Contemporary Views of Theatre For Children," *Educational Theatre Journal*, XXI (1969), pp. 414-425.

Viola, Ann. "Drama With and For Children: An Interpretation of Terms," *Educational Theatre Journal*, VIII (1956), pp. 139-142.

UNPUBLISHED MATERIAL

Hall, Jeanne L. "An Analysis of the Content of Selected Children's Plays with Special Reference to the Developmental Values Inherent in Them." Unpublished Ph.D. Dissertation, The University of Michigan, 1966.